FINDING HIS FIRE

PJ FIALA

DESCRIPTION

When the job is too big for local police, Lynyrd Station calls in the security team. They eliminate the threat when no one else can.

Trailing the arsonist who killed his parents, Ford Montgomery will do anything to take down the entire cartel who ruined his life. But when that trail leads to a sexy waitress who's embroiled in it all, Ford knows he can't turn back now.

Megan Marshall trusts nobody. After all, her ex-husband is a cold-blooded killer--and he's on the loose. So when a hot and rugged Army ranger walks into her life, Megan can't deny the flames that illuminate between them. But their only chance at survival is to take down the deadly cartel that threatens everything. With danger igniting and their passion burning, can the ranger and the waitress extinguish the fire that may engulf them all?

Entire series complete!

USA Today bestselling author PJ Fiala brings you the full and complete Big 3 Security series—heroes willing to sacrifice everything in service to their country, and for the women they love. Full length novel with no cliffhanger, no cheating, and a happily-ever-after guaranteed.

***

Let's stay in contact, join my newsletter so I can let you know about new releases, sales, promotions and more. https://www.subscribepage.com/pjfialafm

CHAPTER 1

Pulling his pickup truck into a parking spot at the edge of the lot, Ford inhaled deeply as he looked at the majestic brick building which had stood longer than any other building in Lynyrd Station. A tornado had swept through town twelve years ago and wiped out most of the town. Few buildings were left fully standing, the courthouse being one of them. Others were partially destroyed and now had new additions added on to the formerly standing walls. So, the courthouse was revered in a special way as indestructible. Today, he only hoped it ended this black chapter in his life.

Spotting his sister, Emmy Lou, and his brother, Dawson, waiting for him at the top of the steps in front of the entrance, he pulled his keys from the ignition and exited his truck. Swallowing the lump in his throat as he neared them, the somber looks on their faces told his story. They were scared, worried, and sick to have to be here today but eager to get on with life. Their new life.

His boots made soft thumping sounds as he ascended the steps to greet his siblings. The sun beat down, already

1

creating a bead of sweat on his temple, and he could feel moisture gather at his back. Another scorcher today.

He hugged Emmy first. Her long, dark hair was pulled back into a ponytail at her nape, her dark eyes so much like his held the emotions of a hundred people in them. He wrapped his arms around her tighter and pulled her closer, whispering in her ear, "We'll be okay. We can do this."

"I know. I'm not used to being on this side of the court-room, and I'm nervous as hell."

"'Bout time you see what some of your clients have to go through. It'll make you a better lawyer for them."

She scoffed and slapped at his shoulder, but the weak smile she gave him said it all. She thought so too. She was a damned good lawyer, though she often found herself working for the worst clients. Drug dealers and pedophiles —as a defense lawyer, she got them all. But she always believed a fair trial kept these scumbags from getting an appeal and kept them in jail where they belonged. Good thing they didn't know she felt that way.

Turning to Dawson, Ford wrapped him in a warm embrace. "Love you, man. It's going to be all right."

"I know, Ford. We're finally going to see this piece of shit go to jail for killing Mom and Dad. I haven't been able to sleep, thinking we'd finally be getting justice for them."

"It's all I've been able to think about for the past four years."

"Yeah, I get that." Dawson, the youngest of the three of them and the most emotional, blinked away the wetness gathering in his eyes. Dawson's sandy brown hair and blue eyes were just like their mom's, and Ford had to swallow the lump that had grown in his throat at the thought. Their parents had been killed in a fire set by Bobby Ray June just over four years ago; he'd been tracking Bobby Ray ever since. Then, Bobby Ray was a suspect in the fires that burned through Gatlinburg and Pigeon Forge, Tennessee, and Ford had been so damned mad that he hadn't gotten to him. He stepped up his efforts which required him to be away from home for five months and finally brought him in eight months ago. Getting to this trial had seemed like an eternity, and his heart was heavy that he hadn't been able to get justice for his parents. That is, until now. Finally.

Stepping back, he inhaled deeply and asked, "Shall we head inside?"

They turned to enter the old brick building, the sun still high in the sky. The cloudless day seemed a good omen for them.

"Ford! Hey, wait up."

He turned to see Detective Rory Richards briskly walking toward them. Leaning forward to shake hands with his high school friend, Ford could see the trouble in his eyes.

"Hey, I hate to be the one to tell you this, and I'm so sorry." He cleared his throat. "Bobby Ray June escaped as he was being transported to court this morning."

"What?" Emmy yelled. "Honest to God, didn't you have that animal chained up in every way possible?"

Tears instantly raced down her cheeks as she looked to Ford for their next move. His jaw clenched, and his heart dropped to the bottom of his stomach, threatening to spill the meager contents inside.

"He had help. We're thinking Waylon June." Rory's fingers shook as he handed the grainy pictures to him. "We'd like you on this, Ford—if you think you want to track this asshole down again."

It was hard to make out distinct features, but the resemblance was certainly the mark of family. Sliding each picture off to Emmy and Dawson as he looked them over, the last one was a gut punch. Both Bobby Ray and Waylon giving the camera on the prison escort van the finger and wearing smiles on their disgusting pudgy faces.

Emmy gasped as she saw the last picture. Dawson swore and choked back a sob. Emmy grabbed Ford's arm and turned him toward her. "You have to go. You have to go and get that motherfucker again."

CHAPTER 2

"Good morning!" she cheerfully said to no one in particular but to all who were within earshot.

"Morning, Megan. I've got your breakfast all ready. It's chicken day, so you're gonna be busy, need to eat to build up your strength." Nila's deep, gravelly voice could be heard over the clatter of dishes and frying foods. A large woman in her early sixties, Nila had hired Megan when she needed a job, and they'd been together for the past four years. Everyone in town loved Nila's broasted chicken and her apple pies. Megan loved that Nila took care of her, and she returned the favor. It wasn't uncommon for Nila to forget to eat herself—especially on chicken day.

"Thank you. I'll just do a quick sweep of the dining room with the coffeepot before I sit."

Tying her spring green apron around her waist, she breezed through the double swinging saloon doors to the dining room and quickly assessed the capacity. About half full now. It wouldn't be long before it would be impossible to hear herself think as it filled with customers, all chatting, laughing, and enjoying the atmosphere. Small town meets southern charm meets the best deal in town—and the best food too. It was a business gold mine.

"Morning, Ralph. Ed. More coffee?" She filled their cups without waiting for them to respond. They always wanted more coffee. Regulars came in at six in the morning and sat through the better part of breakfast, gossiping about who was where and when they came and went. Gossip central right here.

Edging her way through the tables set for four, the red and white upholstered chairs in shiny vinyl and chrome legs resembled a fifties diner. She continued chatting and pouring until she came to a booth in the corner. Stopping short of the table, her stomach plummeted as her eyes caught those of the occupant. Lazar blue eyes trapped her, causing her throat to go dry as her heart sped. Not again. This was the fifth day in a row. Why wouldn't he believe her and go harass someone else?

"Marcus. I don't suppose I could hope that you're actually here for the food today?"

Slowly pushing his cup to the edge of the table, she gritted her teeth as she concentrated on filling it but fantasied about dumping the whole pot over his head.

"I think we both know why I'm here."

Lifting her eyes to his, she slowly inhaled and held her breath for a moment before exhaling.

"I don't know where Waylon is. We're divorced. Have been for over six damned years. He doesn't check in. He doesn't call. He doesn't write. He doesn't visit. And I like it that way. I want nothing to do with him or you or any of your cohorts. Now, if I need to call the police about the harassment, I certainly will."

A smile spread across his face in a slow slither, as if he were a snake—which was the perfect way to describe him.

He was a drug runner, and unfortunately for her, so was Waylon. Also, unfortunately for her, Waylon seemed to have stolen a very valuable something from Marcus, and he wanted it back.

"I think you're blowing this all out of proportion. I'm sitting here drinking coffee, not unlike those gentlemen over there you chatted so nicely with, and I simply ask you a couple of questions about a mutual friend. Don't think the cops are going to be too interested in that story."

She clenched her jaw tightly as her breathing increased.

"Plus, with your record, I don't think the police are going to believe you over me. I don't have a police record."

"Yet," she spat out.

He shrugged.

Turning abruptly, she hustled back to the kitchen, more to get away from him than anything else, but also ... well, to get away from him. Ramming her fists into her apron pockets to hide the shaking from Nila, she walked past the table set with her plate and a fresh glass of orange juice, intending to use the restroom.

"Hey girl, you need to eat," Nila called after her.

Giving a quick wave of her hand and a glance over her shoulder, she replied, "Just gotta use the bathroom. Be back."

Locking the wooden door behind her, she leaned against it, wrapping her hands around her stomach, hoping to quell the roiling. He was right in that he didn't actually do anything to her other than ask questions, but she knew for a fact that he'd followed her home yesterday and the day before. He watched her house most of the night too. She'd gone onto her front porch to water all of her flowers, and there he was, not even hiding the fact that he was watching her. In the middle of the night, she could have sworn she heard footsteps on the porch. Her heart beat so fast, she thought it'd take off and fly away. Listening for the jiggle of the door handle or the rattle of one of her old windows, she was finally able to relax after about an hour when no such sounds reached her ears. She didn't mention it today because she wanted to pretend it wasn't happening, and he wasn't getting bolder. She was probably being stupid. These weren't people you messed with. If she knew where that jackass ex-husband of hers was, she'd turn him over in a heartbeat.

"Megan, honey, time to get rolling. You okay in there?" Nila knocked softly.

"Yes. I'll be right out, Nila."

Washing her hands, she breathed in and out a couple times and told herself it would be all right. Leaving the bathroom, she smoothed down her apron, shoulders back, head high and forced herself to be brave. Then she heard Chad, the busboy, say, "Huh, never seen that guy before."

CHAPTER 3

Shuffling through the pictures once more, Ford stopped on the picture of Megan. Waylon June's ex-wife was a pretty little thing. Green eyes that sparkled at the camera and thick auburn hair trailing to just past her shoulder blades was a stunning combination. Her sweet, perfect smile and smattering of light freckles across her nose spoke of innocence and purity. But you aren't married to a drug dealer and remain pure. Those two things don't go together. And she had an arrest on her record.

He looked up and saw the sign above where she worked: The Log Cabin Restaurant. He shook his head and muttered, "Why in the hell would you work in a restaurant, Megan?"

He glanced through her dossier again. Four years of nursing school. Worked in the field in a hospital for two years, a nursing home for ten, then abruptly quit and began working at The Log Cabin as a waitress. What would make a single woman give up a career where she made good money to sling hash in a little place like that? If her ex was any indicator, she was trouble or looking for it.

Entering the diner, the bell above the door called out his

entrance. A red-haired waitress behind the counter glanced his way and smiled. "Take a seat anywhere you like. One of us will be around with coffee in a minute."

He nodded and glanced to the right. A couple of empty tables sat toward the middle of the dining room and one empty booth toward the window. The booth called his name, so he strode over, slid on the vinyl seat to the middle, and picked up the menu. The smell of bacon and fresh apple pie floated in the air to his nose. He swallowed the lump that formed in his throat. His mom made the best apple pie he'd ever eaten. He loved the spices and cinnamon in her pies, and she always added an extra dash of it for him. He hadn't had apple pie since she died. It was these little things that caught him off guard. Emmy and Dawson, too. They spoke about it every so often, each of them with their own apple pie story.

Glancing around the room and taking in the occupants, he noticed a single gentleman sitting in the corner opposite him and realized he was assessing the room as well. He was by himself in a booth—no food in front of him, just coffee.

Megan walked out of the kitchen, swung past the coffeemaker and began filling the customers' cups. He watched her move, graceful and casual as she gave each patron a bit of attention and a nice smile. She stopped at his table, and he heard her intake of breath when he looked into her eyes. Eyes that, by the way, the picture in his truck did not do justice. Green like a spring day, deep around the outside of the iris, lighter green toward the pupil and hypnotizing. Full lashes framed the green jewels, and he could see she barely wore makeup. Clear skin, faint freckles dusted her nose, and her full sensual lips held just a touch of gloss. *I'll be damned.*

"Care for coffee?" she chirped.

It took him a moment to respond, his mind lagging behind and thinking other thoughts. Clearing his throat, he responded, "Yes. Please."

He turned the cup over that sat on the matching saucer at his place setting and slid it to the edge of the table. He watched as she poured, her arm lifting just enough for him to see the outline of her breast hidden behind her light green apron. It was easy to see what Waylon saw in her, but what in the hell did she see in Waylon? That man was pudgy, unkempt, and a drug dealer. Made no sense.

"Have you had the chance to look at the menu? Special today is chicken if you want to forego breakfast and slide into lunch. Otherwise, we have all the usuals—eggs, bacon, sausage, pancakes, French toast and my favorite, Eggs Benedict."

"Thanks. I'll have two eggs over easy and whole wheat toast. Then, if you'd be so kind, I'd like to know where your ex-husband is."

She stepped back, and he saw her jaw tighten. She practically hissed, "Is this what you two are doing now? You'll keep sending in more and more of you until you're satisfied that I'm not lying?"

"Us two?"

She jerked her head toward the opposite side of the room. "You and Marcus. He's been hounding me all damned week. I'll tell you what I told him—several times." She leaned in, lasered her eyes to his and continued. "I don't know where that useless piece of shit is, and I don't care. I haven't spoken to him in about five years. I don't even have a phone number, and again, I don't want it. If you want your precious item back, go find him. He doesn't come to me and he won't and I sure as hell have no intention of going to him since. I. Don't. Know. Where. He. Is." She finger jabbed the table as she said each syllable as if it made her point clearer.

She straightened her spine and tossed her head in Marcus' direction. Slowly shaking her head back and forth as if to scold him, she turned to him again. "Now, any other way I can make myself clear?"

He straightened his spine, glanced over at Marcus, and then looked into her eyes. "I don't know Marcus. I also don't know about any precious item. What I do know ..." He leaned toward her, set his jaw and locked eyes with her. "... is Waylon helped Bobby Ray June escape from the prison transport van on the way to his trial for killing two people in a fire. I. Want. Waylon. And. Bobby. Ray." He finger jabbed the table just as she had previously, to emphasize *his* point.

Gasping, her free hand flew to her mouth, her eyes closed, and she swallowed. Opening her eyes, she softly asked, "Bobby Ray killed someone?"

"Yes."

"Oh, God."

———

She made her way to the kitchen, her stomach twisted, and she thought she'd lose the little bit of the Eggs Benedict Nila had made for her. Bobby Ray always was a piece of crap. She hated it when he came around. He leered at her and creeped her out. She complained to Waylon about it, and he told her to pull up her big girl panties. Toward the end of their marriage, whenever Bobby Ray would come by, she'd disappear to the grocery store or her best friend, Jolie's, house. She knew he was dangerous and not mentally sound, but she had no idea he was capable of murder.

She tucked her order slip for the gorgeous, but probably dangerous, man in the booth by the window, beneath the spring on Nila's order wheel.

"Order for table eight is up, Megan," Nila called out when she saw her approach. Taking a deep breath, she grabbed the two plates and carried them to the nice couple, asking if they needed a coffee refill.

Keeping herself busy wasn't a problem as the restaurant filled up. "Order up for table seventeen." Squaring her shoulders, she picked up the two eggs over easy and whole wheat toast, grabbed the coffeepot and headed to the table of the man who both excited and scared her. He was a broody sort; his darker than dark eyes were both mesmerizing and scary. They were so dark, it was hard to tell where the iris and pupil met. His strong jaw held a hint of whiskers as if he'd shaved hours ago. The dark shadow gave him a mysterious presence which she bet he loved. She hadn't seen him walk in, but the length of his legs under the table and of his arms on top told her he was tall. From the side, she could see he was fit and firm. Nice. But no. She was steering clear.

"Here you go." Sliding his plate in front of him, she lay his silverware, wrapped in a napkin alongside his plate. "Coffee?" Proud that she was keeping her voice even, she poured when he nodded. Then she watched as his eyes caught movement behind her and his back stiffened. She could feel the heat at her back before she heard Marcus whisper in her ear, "I'm watching you, Megan. You may as well make contact with that jerk you were married to before things get very ugly for you."

Before she could respond, he was gone. Setting the coffeepot on the table before she dropped it, she clasped her hands together in front of her to quell the shaking. He was getting bolder.

Looking up slightly to see what her mysterious man was doing, her heartbeat hitched. Those deep black eyes bored into hers, but this time they held something else. Sympathy? Caring? Probably not, but he didn't look as menacing as he had before.

"Looks like Marcus there is getting bold."

"You don't know the half of it."

"Why don't you tell me?"

She picked up the coffeepot and stepped back. "I don't even know you. Why would I share that kind of thing with a stranger?"

"My name is Ford Montgomery, and I'm here for the same reason Marcus is—to find Waylon. But not for the same reasons. I was hired by the Kane County Police Department to bring him and Bobby Ray in. Looks like we could be friends and help each other out."

Biting her bottom lip, she thought about it. Actually thought about it. His low sexy voice washed over her in a soothing way, and she'd bet her next ten checks he'd lured women of all kind in with those looks and that Sam Elliot voice of his. But, it was too easy to rely on him and too convenient. It would be nice, though, to have someone to turn to.

"Thanks, Ford, for the offer, but I don't think so."

CHAPTER 4

Chicken day flew right by, but man, oh man, she was dog-ass tired. Pulling her sweet little white Jeep Wrangler into her garage, she climbed out and pulled the garage door down behind her. With Marcus and Ford lurking around, she'd need to start closing that door when she left in the morning. It was the first time in all the years she'd lived here that she felt like she had to close the damned garage door. Fucking Waylon and his son of a bitch cousin, Bobby "Fucking" Ray.

Walking to the end of the driveway, she pulled her mail from the mailbox, sifted through the two ads for crafts at the local mall in Harper Valley, around thirty-five miles away, the electric bill, and her favorite country living maga-zine as she walked to the house. Stopping at the bottom step of her porch, she took a moment to admire her little house. It had been her grandmother's house first, but she was mostly raised here after her dad took off and her mom died. She was twelve then. Her brother, Cord, and her sister, Delaney, were six and four years older than her, respec-tively. Cord left home and got a job on an offshore rig the week after he turned eighteen, and Delaney spent most of her time at her boyfriend's house. Though it didn't take him long to dump her when he met the newest blonde with big breasts in town. Cad.

She'd painted the wraparound porch white this summer, and even though it took her the better part of a week to get the whole thing painted, it looked fabulous with its gleaming white spindles and floor. Her brightly colored flower pots and flowers added that homey touch she loved. It looked like one of the pictures she often saw in her country magazine. She should submit a picture of it. Maybe she would once she painted the house yellow this summer. Then, the whole look would be complete.

Entering her clean, fresh living room, she took a deep breath and released it. Home. She placed her magazine on the coffee table with her other magazines, neatly fanning them out to see the titles. She smiled as she walked across the room to her bedroom. Setting her purse on the floor in the closet, she kicked off her shoes. Ahh, that felt heavenly. She pulled the hair band from her ponytail. Scrubbing her head with her fingers to ease the tension from the band and the day, she began to let herself relax.

Making her way back to the coffee table, she picked up the ads and the water bill when she heard a tapping that sounded like something dropping in the kitchen. Her brows furrowed as she listened again, and this time the tapping grew louder. Walking toward the kitchen door, she could smell something—gas, maybe? But before she could get through the door, there was an explosion.

. . .

W aking, she opened her eyes but couldn't see anything. Smoke filled her lungs, and she began coughing. Realization finally sank in, and she felt around her to get her bearings. She was on the living room floor, the coffee table to her right. The roar and crackle finally met her ears, and the direness of the situation wrapped around her, and fear seized her movement. Her heartbeat raced.

As the heat rose in the room, her self-preservation mechanism finally clicked in. She rolled onto her stomach, but coughing threatened to make her pass out. Pulling the neckline of her T-shirt up over her nose and mouth, she found relief, but just a bit. Crawling in the direction she thought led to the front door, relief swept through her when she felt it within reach. Rising up on her knees, she twisted the handle and found it locked. Panicking, she tried over and over to twist the handle and find the lock. The heat was increasing, and the orange of the flames began to poke through the gray, smoke-filled room.

"Help!" she yelled but began coughing again.

Hitting her fists against the door, she tried again. "Help!"

"Megan? Unlock the door."

Frozen in fear at the voice on the other side, she shook her head, but help was help, and she needed it.

CHAPTER 5

From his truck two doors down, he watched Megan close her garage door, rubbing her back as she made her way to her mailbox. He'd watched the diner most of the day and assumed she'd run her little legs off—figuring the whole of South Pass must have come through the doors of the Log Cabin at least once. The food was fantastic, and many left with Styrofoam boxes filled with all they couldn't eat.

He watched as she admired the front of her house and then stepped inside. Settling back into the seat of his truck, he logged onto his laptop and checked his email while often glancing toward her house. If he was lucky, Waylon would show up looking for help from Megan, and he could nab him and save her from Marcus at the same time. Not that she'd asked. But, he could tell she was afraid of Marcus, and if he was honest, that was another reason he was sitting here now. It went against his grain to see a woman in need and not help her, and he'd bet his whole paycheck that she needed help.

An explosion sounded, and when he looked up, he saw the smoke coming from the back of Megan's house. Quickly jumping from his truck, he ran across the street. He could hear her coughing and trying to twist the door handle.

"Megan? Unlock the door."

"It's stuck. I can't."

He heard her fall into a fit of coughing and looked around the porch for something to throw through the front window. Seeing a pot filled with colorful flowers, he shook his head and picked it up.

"Back away from the window," he yelled through the door.

He hefted the large pot to shoulder height and tossed it through the window.

He heard her gasp but didn't stop to wait. Using his boot, he swiped the broken glass from the bottom and sides of the window as much as he could and folded himself through it.

Running his hand along the wall, he held his T-shirt over his nose and mouth with the other, inching his foot in front of him, so he didn't step on her.

"Megan, where are you? We need to get out of here." He tried keeping the fear from his voice but felt he was losing that battle.

Coughing sounded next to him, and he reached down with both hands and found her shoulders. He scooped her up and slid along the wall to the window. The smoke was so thick, it was impossible to see anything but the bit of light streaming through where he'd just come in and the orange flames racing toward them.

Bending down, he threw one long leg through the window, ducked a bit farther and stepped out onto the porch. But he didn't stop until they were at the edge of the yard.

Sirens wailed in the distance as he laid her on the grass, her coughing still heavy, but her lungs would hopefully clear soon.

Smoothing her hair away from her face, his heart hurt for her. This woman had been through a lot this week—probably her whole life, but this week he knew for sure had been stressful, if Marcus' comments were any indicator.

Her coughing subsided as the fire trucks pulled up.

"Sir, you're going to need to get out of the way; we need you over by that pickup truck," a fireman yelled.

Easily picking her up, Ford carried her across the street. She tried protesting, but her voice was raspy, and her lungs were still heavy with smoke, so the words came out garbled.

"Shh. It's okay, Megan. I won't hurt you."

Her eyes opened, and the bright green he'd seen earlier hadn't dimmed, though the whites of her eyes were now reddened from the smoke. Their eyes locked, and he saw when she'd finally stopped wrestling with herself as her features relaxed. Then he noticed his heart raced just a bit faster as he looked into those green eyes. Her tongue swiped across her bottom lip, leaving a glossy path, and he shook his head to clear it of sensual thoughts, which wasn't easy with her soft body pressed against his.

He laid her on the ground and seconds later an ambulance pulled to the curb directly in front of them. Two paramedics came to their side; one immediately began pulling items from a bag, and the other shined a light into her pupils to see them dilate.

"Megan, are you all right? Besides the smoke you inhaled, did you hit your head or hurt yourself in any way?"

She nodded. Coughed a bit more and rasped out, "I

think I hit my head on the floor when the explosion happened. Knocked out a bit." More coughing.

One of the attendants covered her nose and mouth with an oxygen mask and said, "Okay, just relax and take in this oxygen to help you breathe."

A blood pressure cuff was placed on her arm while the other attendant listened to her lungs, asking her to breathe in and out slowly, so she didn't make herself cough.

Unable to look away, he watched her as she complied with every request they made of her. Breathe in and out. Look up. Show me where you hit your head. On and on and without a peep of complaint.

"Meg, do you want me to call Delaney or Cord?"

She shook her head no, the mask still covering her mouth.

"You sure? They'll be pissed if they find out you didn't call. Cord, especially."

She shook her head again, and Ford wondered who Delaney and Cord were. No mention of them in her file.

The two attendants then turned to him. "You all right, mister?"

He nodded. "Yes, I'm fine."

"You have blood on your arm. I'd like to take a look at it, if you don't mind."

Glancing down at the blood that had dribbled down his forearm, his brow furrowed. He hadn't noticed that at all; he'd been so wrapped up in Megan.

Nodding at the attendant, he held his arm out and only winced once when he applied something to the cut that stung, then quickly bandaged it. "Not too deep but keep it clean and covered for a couple of days."

"Thanks."

Glancing back to Megan, she'd sat up and watched as they bandaged his arm.

"Megan? You want to go to the hospital for a checkup?"

"No." Clearing her throat, she looked at the attendant. "Thanks, Jason. Tell Susannah I said hello."

"Will do, Meg. You make sure you call Cord, so I don't get an ass chewing next time he comes home."

That made her smile. "I'll call him; now, go on home."

The two attendants packed up their supplies and spoke to one of the firefighters and a cop before they took off. As the ambulance pulled away, the look on Megan's face was pitiful indeed. She looked at her house across the street, now soot-stained and blackened, water still raining in through the windows in the kitchen on both sides from the firemen's hoses.

The tear stains were difficult to hide as they cleaned a trail down her soot-dirtied cheeks. She swallowed hard as she smudged the dampness from her face, seemingly trying to comprehend what had just happened.

And, dammit, his heart hurt for her. Kneeling down next to her, he swiped her hair back from her cheek, enjoying the softness of it between his fingers. "Where can I take you tonight? Do you have a place to stay?"

Turning her head to him, her brows furrowed for a moment, then she frowned. "I guess I can call my friend, Jolie, and see if she can let me sleep on her sofa tonight."

He pulled his phone from his back pocket and handed it to her. "Give her a call, and I'll take you there."

"I need to get some things from inside."

He shook his head. "You won't be allowed inside tonight, Megan. They need to put the fire out, and then they'll need to do an investigation to see what started it. Did you hear anything prior to the explosion?"

Her brows furrowed slightly as she tried remembering. "I heard clicking or tapping, like something small fell and bounced on the floor. I was going in to investigate what that sound was, but the explosion happened and threw me back into the living room."

"Okay." He squeezed her shoulder. "They'll figure it out. Give your friend a call."

He stood to give her some privacy, but she stopped him. "Where are you going?" She almost sounded panicked.

"Nowhere, hon. I'll be right here." His heart thudded in his chest as he watched her—spoke to her. She truly seemed like a woman caught up in the middle of something she had no part in creating.

Nodding, she swiped the screen on his phone, saw that it needed a password and held it out to him with a small trembling smile.

He touched his forefinger to the button on the bottom, and it opened up. He watched her shaky fingers dial her friend's number and then swallow before putting the phone to her ear. Her lips quivered as she said, "Jolie." Voice cracking, she swallowed again, gaining her composure. "My house burned down. Can I stay at your house tonight?"

More tears followed the former trails, and she angrily swiped them. He tuned out but stayed close as he took in the sight of the house. It wouldn't be habitable for a long time, and if this was arson, she wasn't safe here. His gut told him it was, and his gut was seldom wrong. His gut also told him only two people would have tried to kill Megan. Marcus seemed to be getting bolder, and Bobby Ray June was known for setting fires and killing people. Especially if he thought Megan had talked to Marcus about something. Bobby Ray would certainly know that Waylon took something he wasn't supposed to have and both men were running from the law and other unsavory characters—the only one they knew of for sure being Marcus. Two dangerous, scared men on the loose was never a good thing, and Megan knew both men. So the question of the day was, how well did she know them now and why would they want her dead?

CHAPTER 6

Ford was there when the explosion happened, yet she didn't think he'd set the fire, so that meant he'd been watching her house. Marcus had been watching her house too, but that felt creepy somehow. The thought of Ford watching her didn't feel creepy at all.

She had to admit, when she'd heard his voice calling to her when she couldn't get out of the house, she was scared at first and then so damned relieved it wasn't Marcus. When he picked her up and carried her out of the house, the first thought that came to her was a knight in shining armor. Though he was no knight and she wasn't a damsel. Far from it.

He hadn't even known he cut himself coming through the window. Had he been worried about her? So gentle and kind afterward, it made her head hurt. Men weren't usually nice to her. They sure as hell never stuck around to help her. Her father, her brother, Waylon. All of them took off early and left her to fend for herself. So, it was only a matter of time, and Ford would leave too.

She took his proffered phone to call her best friend, Jolie.

Ford stepped back, and she almost panicked and asked him where he was going. When he said, "Nowhere, hon," she had to swallow the lump that formed. She hadn't been called "hon" in a long damned time, and that nearly cracked her. Then she heard Jolie answer the phone and that's when she almost broke down. Hearing Jolie's compassion and caring brought home all that had happened and had been happening to her this past week. A hug from Jolie and her adorable kids, a good night's sleep, and she'd be ready to face the world tomorrow. Jolie's husband, Derek, always made sure his family was buttoned up tight for the night and safe and sound. Something she'd never had, except for when she stayed at her friend's house. Yeah, she'd feel so much better in the morning.

She tapped the end call icon and looked up at Ford who stood sentry by her, but looked far, far away. He stared at her house like he was waiting for the answer to a question. She had just a moment to admire all that was Ford Montgomery—tall and broad shouldered. He had the sleeves of his gray button-up shirt rolled to his elbows. Sexy forearms showed chiseled muscles so firm the veins stood out against them. Shit, what was it about a man's forearms that could make her drool?

Taking a deep breath and marveling that she didn't fall into a fit of coughing, she twisted her head and took in all that was left of her house. It was the only thing her grandmother had to give her—her childhood home. That and the diamond cross necklace that she cherished. She'd certainly need to go back into the house for that. Maybe by morning, they'd let her in. Hopefully, it hadn't been damaged. Sadness washed over her as dawning began sinking in. Everything she owned was in that house. Even her purse was in there. Her phone. Everything likely damaged or gone.

Tears sprang to her eyes again, but she clenched her jaw and angrily swiped them away. Nope. She'd been through worse than this; she'd manage. She just needed to make sure Marcus wasn't trying to kill her and that she didn't get too close to Ford and get her stupid heart broken. In that order.

CHAPTER 7

Rotating his head to release the stiffness, Ford continued to shift his gaze from Jolie's house to the sleek black Mercedes slowly driving past at regular intervals. He'd caught a glimpse of the driver the last time he drove past. Luckily, he wasn't looking at the truck but was keeping his eyes trained on Jolie's house. Not that he could have seen inside with the darkened windows he'd spent large bills on. It was a business expense.

Glancing in the outside mirrors, he made sure Marcus' car turned the corner and knew he'd be back in about twenty minutes. Pulling his phone up, he tapped a couple of icons and located Detective Richard's phone number. Tapping the phone icon, he rested the phone against his right ear, keeping his eyes on Jolie's house.

"Any word?" Typical Richards, short and to the point.

"Maybe. I need you to run a plate for me. Illinois - NTP-823. Black Mercedes around 2016."

Tapping sounded in the background, and he knew his friend was on it. "What else is going on?"

"Well, Megan June has her hands full. Some asshole named Marcus—"

"Marcus Salsado," his friend finished.

"What else do you know?"

"No record. But he's rumored to be a manager for the El Pablo Cartel. Small time manager and he seems to be located in the Midwest. But, up till now, he's managed to keep his hands clean. The only reason he's on police radar is that he was the owner of a house that burned down a few months back where a bunch of whores were found packing blow. He got off without charges because he produced a lease that showed he wasn't the occupant at the time. One Brandon Garcia was the tenant. However, Marcus is being watched because mysteriously, Mr. Garcia has never been found."

Ford's jaw tightened. "Any word that Waylon June would be involved with Marcus or Brandon Garcia?"

A bit more tapping came over the line, and Ford straightened when he saw the front door to Jolie's house open, and a blond man stepped outside. He glanced from side to side, looked down the street both ways, then went back inside.

"Nope. Haven't been able to make a connection there."

"Thanks, Rory."

"Hey, stay sharp out there. Still no sightings of Bobby Ray or Waylon June. Those bastards are lurking around somewhere."

"You too. Let me know if anything comes to light. In the meantime, I'm working this angle here." He heard Rory's chuckling on the line before he disconnected. Asshole.

Glancing at the time on his phone, he saw his night was just beginning. He reached for his thermos of coffee, poured himself a shallow cup, inhaled the fresh aroma of the caramel brew he'd purchased just for this stakeout, then sipped the piping hot liquid.

———

By the time five o'clock in the morning came, Marcus had practically worn a path in the street driving past, and Ford had listened to a whole book on tape. The story was good too. *The Appeal* by John Grisham. He devoured those books.

Sitting behind his darkened windows, knowing Marcus had spotted the truck but couldn't see him inside, he waited for Marcus to turn the corner once again and then exited his truck and walked to the front door of Jolie's house. He knocked on the door and the same blond man that had stepped outside last night came to the door.

"How can I help you?"

He held out his hand. "My name's Ford Montgomery. I'd like to see Megan if she's awake."

The man looked into his eyes for a long time, then finally turned when Megan approached from behind and said, "It's okay, Derek, I'll talk to him."

Derek's lips thinned to a straight line, but he stepped back and let Megan into the opening of the door. His heartbeat actually picked up when he saw her. Freshly showered and wearing a pair of jeans and a scoop neck T-shirt in light pink, she looked sweet and innocent. Her hair was pulled up into a ponytail on the top of her head, its thick auburn length sweeping over her shoulder—the ends curling perfectly at the tip just above her breast.

"Morning." Her voice sounded rested but a bit raspy. Probably from all the smoke yesterday.

"Good morning. Wonder if we might have a little chat."

"I don't know where Way—"

Holding up a hand to stop her, he cut her off. "I don't want to talk about Waylon. But, we do need to either go inside or out back where we're hidden from the street."

"Why?"

"Honey, you're in a bit of trouble here, and I'd like to help you. Do you actually know who Marcus is?"

He saw her swallow hard but still hesitate. "He's been driving past this house every twenty minutes most of the night. There were about two hours where he didn't, but otherwise, he's watching this place, and that means if we're standing here, he'll see both of us."

She stepped back and allowed him to enter the house. Behind him, she twisted a deadbolt lock on the door and then motioned for him to follow her to the kitchen.

"Can I get you some coffee?"

"Naw, I've had quite a bit over the night."

"I saw your truck outside all night. Why did you stay outside and watch the house? I told you Waylon wouldn't come to me."

"Because I had a sneaking suspicion you needed someone watching out for you. Marcus is eager to watch you, and from what I've been able to gather from my contacts, he's dangerous."

CHAPTER 8

"How dangerous?" She asked the question, but she knew or had a pretty good idea. Waylon stole something from Marcus and knowing Waylon, it was either money or drugs, and she'd bet her next month's paycheck it was drugs. Waylon, for all his faults, always thought if he could just get a chance, he'd be big time. No matter that big time for Waylon was still doing something illegal. He dreamed of running a crew and making more money than he could ever spend. Highly unlikely; the man spent every penny that passed through his hands.

"He's suspected of being involved with the El Pablo Cartel in Medellin, Mexico. They're a rival faction to the Medellin Cartel and stupid enough to think they can take over drug operations down there. The Medellin Cartel is deadly, well ingrained in the system, and owns more cops and court officials than a mathematician can count, so it's highly unlikely."

She swallowed. Well, now that was more than she knew or cared to know. "Um ..." Licking the dryness away from her lips, she looked into his eyes. Dark and mysterious, he could look totally menacing and damned sexy at the same time. His dark hair held a sheen to it and her fingers itched to touch it. As he stood here before her, he exuded a raw power and strength. He'd been sitting in a truck all night, yet he didn't look bedraggled and worn. His strong jaw once again held that hint of a shadow from not shaving, which added to his mysterious image.

"Well, I guess I'm not surprised that Waylon would be hooked up with someone like that. But, I'm not going to lie, it scares me and pisses me off at the same time."

"Here's the thing, Megan. With or without knowing it, he's dragged you into it. Marcus isn't likely to stop following you. I'm not a hundred percent certain he didn't set your house on fire. I don't know who did, but I'll bet you someone did. So, you've got a potential drug cartel following you, maybe trying to hurt or kill you. Do you have a plan moving forward?"

Jolie stepped into the kitchen, a towel wrapped around her hair. She wore jeans and a loose-fitting top, but she looked fresh and wholesome. Her blue eyes landed on Ford, and Megan watched her friend look him from head to toe without saying a word. When she turned, Jolie looked her way, brows high in the air and a slight smile on her lips. She could see the wheels turning.

"Good morning." Stepping toward Ford, she held her hand out. "I'm Jolie."

"Ford."

They shook hands, and Jolie walked to the coffeepot, giving her a sidelong glance that said far more than words ever could. Ford was sexy. He filled the kitchen with more than just his physical presence. He had an authority about him that couldn't be denied. It was comforting, like a warm blanket wrapping itself around her shoulders.

"So, I got up a few times during the night and noticed your truck sitting a couple of doors down. What's up?"

She leaned against the counter, coffee cup raised to sip, eyes locked on Ford's.

He straightened and slipped the first two fingers of each hand into his front jeans pockets. "I was just talking to Megan about that. She needs to be in a safe house, out of sight and safe until authorities can figure out who set her house on fire and find Waylon June."

Jolie lowered her coffee cup and turned toward her. "They know it was arson?"

"No. Ford just thinks so."

"We'll know soon enough, and I have a call into the fire department. I'd bet my life on it."

"Meg? What's going on? What has that asshole gotten you involved in this time?"

Rubbing the nape of her neck and rotating her head, she softly stated, "It appears he stole something from a drug cartel."

"That son of a bitch. He's just got to go. He's not even around, and he's getting you into trouble again. What the fuck?"

"Hey! Kids," Derek said sharply as he entered the kitchen, their youngest daughter, Sarah Jo, on his hip.

"Momma said a bad word." The little three-year-old giggled and covered her mouth with her tiny hands.

"Yes, and I'm very sorry. Let's get you some breakfast." Jolie took her daughter from her husband and settled her at the table. Catching Ford's gaze, Megan nodded toward the living room. Instinctively, upon entering the room, she glanced out the window and saw Marcus' car round the corner, having just passed the house. Again.

"I don't have anywhere to go, Ford." She let the curtain fall once again and turned to face him.

"You don't have family somewhere who can help you?"

She shook her head. Her brother was on an offshore oil rig somewhere, and her sister hadn't spoken to her for six years since she'd inherited her grandmother's house—the house that was now a pile of ashes. Ironic.

"I know a place. It's only about ninety miles from here. Safe, secluded, and no one will know you're there. It's clean and private, but great visibility, should someone try to get close to the house."

She looked into his eyes and saw sincerity, but why was he helping her? "Right. Don't tell me, let me guess; it's your house?"

The corner of his sexy lips tipped up. "Sort of. Used to be, I guess. It's vacant now, and it's safe. Do I need to remind you that you have nowhere else to go?"

She took in a deep breath and let it out slowly to keep her heart from beating out of her chest. Panicking right now was not a great idea. Suddenly, her peaceful life was falling apart in a sea of chaos and deep shit. Fucking Waylon.

"Megan." She looked up at him, again taken with his presence. "You can't put Jolie and her family in danger."

Glancing toward the kitchen, her heart sank. He was right about that. She probably already had put them in the sights of Marcus. That was stupid.

"He knows where they live." She fought the tears that threatened.

"We can let him follow us for a bit. He'll know you aren't here and perhaps keep looking for you or focus on Waylon once you're gone."

"How do you know?"

"You don't have a choice, Megan." He stepped closer to

her, and she could smell him. His scent was leather and woodsy and so masculine. It fit him so perfectly.

"Why do you care?" She refused to step back and make him think he intimidated her, even though she *was* a little intimidated. The way things worked in her life, he'd begin to help her, then disappear like every other man in her life, so she looked at his chest to keep her focus.

"Look." His strong, firm fingers cupped her chin and lifted her face up to look into his eyes. "I have a stake in getting Waylon and Bobby Ray, but that doesn't mean I'd throw you or anyone else to the wolves to get them. And, look around, Meg. You don't have anyone else."

Dammit. He was right, and if she was honest with herself, he *did* make her feel more secure. He didn't seem to let people bowl him over, and one dark stare from those black eyes of his would make a wolf cower.

"What's your stake?"

"Really?" He crossed his arms over his chest and widened his stance. He looked battle ready. "You're in a shit ton of trouble with a drug cartel, and you really give a shit about my stake?"

His phone rang, but he never looked away from her as he pulled it from his back pocket. "Yeah." His low sexy voice floated around her. She had no choice.

"Okay. I'm taking care of it." He put his phone back in his pocket. "Gotta run, Megan. Time isn't on our side."

CHAPTER 9

He felt sorry for Megan. She had no one. She had nowhere to go, and by the looks of things, she didn't have a ton of money to get her through hiding out safely. But why in the fuck did he offer up his house? There is definitely something wrong with his brain right now. Must be from sitting in a truck all night.

Trying to reason his motives out now wasn't going to work. Not when he could smell her shower fresh skin next to him, and every time he glanced at her, she licked her lips. She didn't mean for it to be, but it was sensual in an innocent sort of way that was beginning to affect his nether region. That couldn't happen.

"I want to stop by the house first, please. I need to see if I can get my purse. And my grandmother's necklace."

"Your purse is going to smell of smoke and be useless to you. Why do you need a necklace to hide out?" Typical woman, totally vain.

"It's all I have." She stopped, and he could tell she was fighting emotion. "Of her. The house and the necklace were all I had of my grandma. Now all I have is the necklace."

Oh, not vain—sentimental. Shit!

"You're living in your grandmother's house?"

She nodded as she glanced out the side window. The sun streaming in created a mirror effect, and he could see the moisture in her eyes.

"When she passed, she gave me the house because I took care of her when she was dying. My sister was too busy climbing the corporate ladder, and my brother left town as soon as he turned eighteen and lives on an offshore rig off the coast of California. It was just Grandma and me for years." She cleared her throat and straightened her spine. "Now, it's just me."

She turned to face him, her eyes glistening, but her back was straight and her shoulders squared. "I'm not going to let Waylon get me in trouble and take the last little bit I have of my grandmother. She'd be rolling in her grave. She always hated that asshole."

"Okay. Now you're talking. So, let's get you to safety, and then we'll figure out how to get that son of a bitch out of your life and in jail, and Bobby Ray right along with him."

"Are you a cop or something? Why do you want them?"

"I'm a bounty hunter, and Bobby Ray killed my parents. Waylon broke him out of the prison transport van on the way to his trial. I want both of them."

Her features softened, and sadness filled her eyes. "I'm sorry," she all but whispered. "I didn't know."

Clenching his jaw, he quickly glanced at her. She stood, trying to remain stoic but looked lost and confused.

"It was four years ago, but I think of them every day. Especially now. I need justice for them and my siblings. And I'm going to get it."

———

They pulled up to the curb across from her house, and she sucked in a big breath at the sight of the bedraggled broken mess that used to be her home. The white exterior was charred over most every surface. Her gorgeous flowers on the porch and around the landscaping of the house had been trampled, burned, or blasted by the fire hoses trained on them. Yellow crime scene tape wrapped itself around the house and the garage. Her front door stood at a sickly angle as someone had broken it to get in.

"Oh my God," she whispered. "It's a complete mess."

Without thinking, he reached over and wrapped his fingers around her nape and squeezed gently. Her dainty neck was warm to the touch—her slender shoulders strong and firm under his forearm.

"I'm sorry, Megan. It looks bad now, but once you settle things with your insurance company, you can rebuild. It'll look good as new, and all remnants of the fire will be gone."

"It won't be the same." She turned to look into his eyes, and he was taken with the shade of green that hit him. Earnest and sweet, she certainly seemed to be just that, but something Jolie said kept ringing in his head. *That son of a bitch! He's just got to go. He's not even around, and he's getting you into trouble again. What the fuck?*

He'd bet that was the arrest on her record. He'd need to call Rory a little later and get that information.

"Can we go in?"

"No, not without permission." He pulled his phone from his back pocket and googled the South Pass Fire Department. He tapped the phone icon and called them. When he got the chief on the phone, he explained who he was and asked for permission to enter the house. The chief asked them to wait until he arrived, so here they sat. And as if there were a radar on their presence, Marcus pulled up to the curb in front of the house.

"Figures he'd be here," she snapped. "Look at him look at us."

"He can't see us. I have a coating on the windows that makes it almost impossible to see in. It's mirrored on the outside, so if he's looking at anything, he's staring at himself. Figures he's a narcissist too."

The fire chief pulled into the driveway, and he squeezed her neck with his fingers. "Chief's here. Let's go. Stay close to me, and don't let Marcus get you alone anywhere."

She sucked in a deep breath and reached for the door handle. "Hold up. I'll get it." His brows furrowed. She wasn't used to a man opening doors for her.

Exiting his truck, he walked around the front of it, two-finger saluted Marcus and opened the passenger door, reached in to help Megan down, and wrapped his fingers around hers as they walked to the chief. Marcus exited his car and followed them up the driveway, and her fingers tightened on his.

Keeping his voice low, he said, "It's okay."

The chief greeted them alongside his truck and nodded. "I'm sorry about all of this, Megan. It sure is a shame. Ms. Gladys was a special lady, and this house has been in your family since she was first married to Mr. Marshall."

"Yeah. She loved this house. It's just so sad to see it like this." She turned to face the chief. "Do you know if it was arson?"

"Yes ma'am, we're certain of it. There was an accelerant used in the kitchen in front of the stove. That clicking you heard was likely a lighter or flint block to set it off."

"So, someone was in the house while I was in there?"

The chief's lips thinned into a straight line. "I'm afraid it's very likely."

"Oh, God." She shivered, and he pulled her into his body, encircling his arm around her shoulders. A strange sensation filtered through him when her arms wrapped around his waist.

"I can let you in for only a minute, and you'll only be able to enter the living room and the bedroom; the floor isn't safe in the kitchen. And you'll have to promise not to touch anything other than grabbing your purse and your necklace that Mr. Montgomery mentioned you were looking for."

Nodding her head, she pulled away from him and started toward the house. Marcus had been leaning against the back of the chief's truck, listening and not saying a word. Giving him a long look—his worst look which usually made bigger men than him quiver in their boots—only elicited a smirk from Marcus, which Ford thought was rather curious. Then again, he was usually in the presence of drug lords, so a lowly bounty hunter was likely not scary.

The chief glanced at Marcus then. "Are you with them?"

"No," Ford quickly stated.

"You'll need to stay outside then."

"No problem." His tone was flat, but he looked at Megan when he spoke, and that irritated Ford more than him being here.

He turned and quickly followed Megan and the chief up the steps and watched as the chief lifted the door aside. "Stay to the edges close to the walls where the floor is safer."

Megan's gasp drew his attention. Her hand covered her mouth, her eyes glistening as the tears gathered. All her furniture was water-soaked and charred—the walls as well. The heavy thickness of the air inside was almost suffocating. Between the fire smell and the humidity of the water, mixed with the rising heat outside, this place wouldn't be habitable for a good long time.

"Oh my God, it's gone!"

CHAPTER 10

The drawer where she kept her grandmother's necklace was opened and the contents emptied. "It's gone. Someone stole it."

"Are you sure it was here yesterday when you got home?"

"I'm sure..." She frantically looked around her bedroom and then tried remembering what she did when she got home yesterday. She'd come into the bedroom, dropped her purse into the closet, took off her shoes, removed her hair band, but she hadn't looked at the beside tables. "I don't know," she said dejectedly.

"Okay, and you're sure it was in that night stand and nowhere else?" the chief gently asked her.

What was worse, these two men looked at her as if they didn't believe her or that she was mistaken. She seldom left things out of place; neat and tidy was her thing.

"I'm very tidy. I keep everything in its place. I don't just let things lay around. I'm positive." She swallowed the panic that threatened to break her down. She glanced at Ford and saw that he was looking around the room as if to find something out of place and prove her wrong. Or maybe just looking around. A blush tinted her cheeks as she realized she was standing in her bedroom with two men. One of them, incredibly attractive and mysterious and sexy and ... Shaking her head and closing her eyes, she took a calming breath. She let it out slowly and opened her eyes to see both men staring at her.

"Megan." Ford stepped toward her, his face showing concern. "Is there anywhere else it could be? Please check all of your drawers, anywhere you think it might be."

Walking to her closet, she picked up her purse from the floor, happy to see it wasn't soaked like most of the house. She pulled a few items of clothing from the closet. She'd wash them when she got to where they were going and looked in the built-in drawers in the closet; nothing in there. Picking up a canvas bag from the shelf above the drawers, she added her under garments, the clothing she picked out and a pair of tennis shoes. Stepping from the closet with her bag and her purse, she turned to her dresser and pulled open the top drawer. That was possibly the only other place her necklace could be.

"It's not here. It's gone. Someone took it." Sadness fell over her so cold and dark she thought she'd never feel light and happy again. Everything from her grandmother was completely gone. Wiped from the earth like she'd never even lived. How does that happen when a person had lived for more than eighty-three years?

"Megan, honey, we have to go." Ford was still there watching her try not to crumble. She looked up from her dresser and into his eyes, and it was there that she saw a softness she'd never believed could be there. All his hardness and sternness had faded into the blackened walls of what was left of her house, and a different man stood before her.

"Okay." She led the way out of her bedroom through the living room, staying close to the walls as directed earlier and stepped onto her porch, which just last year she'd so lovingly painted and now it was ruined. Grandma must be so sad.

She walked down the driveway, feeling as though she were having an out-of-body experience and she wasn't really herself. Walking past Marcus, she felt nothing, not even when he quietly said, "I'll be watching you, Megan. Waylon's certainly going to come looking to take care of you now."

She kept walking straight to Ford's truck and stood to wait for him to catch up to her.

"You okay, Meg?"

"Yes. We should put my bag and purse in the box of the truck, so they don't smell up the cab. Do you mind?"

"No, I don't mind, but let's do this right and turn your phone off so we can't be tracked." He unlocked the tonneau cover and lifted the lid, then gently took her bags from her shoulder and set them inside. She reached in and pulled her phone from her purse, held the power button in until it began to shut off, then she gently tossed it back into her purse.

Closing the lid, he gently clutched her shoulders and turned her to the passenger side of the truck. He opened the door and helped her inside. "Buckle up."

She watched him walk in front of the truck and admired his strength. If she were honest with herself, she was grateful for it now. But she'd be careful not to rely on him too much. She'd need to keep her distance, so she didn't fall for him. That wouldn't do; then he'd go away for sure.

"You're safe now, Megan. Marcus may follow us for a while, but we'll make sure he's waylaid soon enough and unable to follow. Okay?"

True to his word, about twenty miles from town, Ford called someone and told them where they were and gave them a description of Marcus' car. It wasn't more than five minutes later, and a cop pulled onto the highway behind Marcus and turned on the lights. She watched this mostly from the side mirror just outside of her window. Seeing Marcus pull over to the curb, she twisted in the seat and glanced out the back window. Holy hell!

Turning forward, she looked at the side of Ford's face, the hint of a smile on his lips. "We're safe now." His sexy voice floated over her, and she had the weirdest sensation of a warm blanket wrapping itself around her.

"How did you do that?"

His smile grew into a stunning transformation of his face for the second time today. Wow!

"I know people."

"Right. But how powerful are these people?"

He gave her a sidelong glance and chills ran through her. Had she mentioned that she thought he was handsome? The realization of all that was him, sitting this close to her and those looks she swore she saw him give her, sent a thrill through her.

"My years as a bounty hunter have put me in touch with many people in law enforcement, so you decide how powerful they are." He turned back to watching the road, but often glanced in the rearview mirror. After a mile or so, he continued, "Besides, asking someone to stop a known associate with a drug cartel isn't calling in a huge favor." He smiled, though it was fleeting. She settled into the seat and watched the scenery fly past the window, the sun shining high in the May sky. Her thoughts ran through her mind faster than the trees and buildings outside the truck.

Ford leaned forward and turned the radio on. "What do you like to listen to?"

Her head still resting on the headrest, she rolled to face him. "Anything Bob Seger or classic rock and some of the newer country. What do you like to listen to?"

"About the same. Throw in some AC/DC and a bit of Zeppelin, and I'm a happy man."

"Seems like we're well matched."

The glance he gave her settled low in her core. She watched his jaw tighten and his Adam's apple bob but tried not to think of what any of that meant. She shouldn't have said that but trying to backtrack now seemed stupid and maybe insulting, so she opted to be quiet.

Calculating the distance they'd traveled and the total trip, she figured they were within twenty miles of their destination. He'd said ninety miles. Nerves began tightening in her gut, and her breathing grew shallow. Maybe she was making a mistake; she didn't know him at all. As she now sat thinking about it, she'd agreed to come with him because she didn't think she had any other choice; yes, she oddly felt safe with him, but now she realized they'd be in a house where no one would know where to find her, and he seemed to just control everything about the situation. What if this was some crazy master plan? He could be anyone at all, and she'd done nothing to research anything about him.

Her fingers twisted painfully in her lap. Her breathing shallowed and she fought the panic by swallowing rapidly. Her purse was in the box of the truck, so she had no money save for her tips from yesterday, which was a good day, but, still ... And for that matter, her phone was back there too.

"What's making you panic right now?"

"Nothing."

"Clearly not nothing. So, let's talk it out."

She swallowed again, looked out the side window and softly stated, "I don't know you or anything about you."

"Hm." He navigated a turn off the highway and reset the cruise. "Not much to tell, really. I lost my parents four years ago. My family wants justice for them, and so do I."

"But that doesn't tell me much. I mean, it does, but why are you helping *me*?"

That was the real question. It simply made no sense that a stranger would care about her or her situation. She had only had one interaction with him before the fire, and now suddenly, he was spiriting her away to safety.

"You're all alone. You're in trouble. You need someone to help you."

Twisting in her seat, she looked at his face. The sun streaming in through the window highlighted his eyes. The blackness took on a whole new look in the light. Not so dark and mysterious but shiny and ... beautiful. He had thick lashes and a strong, firm jawline. His classic nose and cheekbones showed great bone structure. From her nurse's perspective, he was healthy and strong. A great specimen to mate with and bare children; that is, if she were looking.

"Right. But why do you feel compelled to be the person to help me?"

CHAPTER 11

Wasn't that the million-dollar question?

Navigating another corner, he turned off the county road and onto a smaller gravel road that looked like it went right up the mountain. She stopped studying him and began to examine the scenery around them.

"Look, Megan. I know this seems weird, but my job puts me in contact with many bad people. I've seen the likes of the Marcuses, the Waylons, and unfortunately, the Bobby Ray Junes of the world. I get that they prey on people who've done nothing wrong except being in the wrong place at the wrong time. This time, I'm in a position to help one of those people. It's not that big of a deal. At my heart, I'm a good person from a good family, and my parents raised me well."

As they meandered along the road, she gripped the edge of the seat tightly as some portions of the road seemed like it'd lead them right off the side of the mountain, tumbling down to their death. The only comfort was the trees that began crowding the edge on the downslope, which felt like a cocoon enveloping them between the mountain and the trees. Small comfort if they careened off the road and down the side, but she'd think of something else.

"Look up instead of down; it's not as scary."

Now he could read her thoughts. Great.

"How much farther?"

"One more corner and we're good."

Turning the wheel to maneuver them around the side of the hill, a large gate came into view and beyond that, a picturesque ranch home seemed to jut from the side of the mountain as if it were a part of it. Designed of wood and sided to look much like the very trees that surrounded it, it blended so well that from the bottom it would be hard to spot. Stopping at the gate, Ford rolled his window down, reached into a box at the edge of the fence and entered a code on a hidden keypad. The gates popped open and allowed them entry.

"Wow." It came out before she could stop it.

"We're safe here. As you can see," he pointed down the mountain from where they were, "it's nearly impossible to get up here without being noticed. And, once someone makes it this far, they'd need a code. The only people with the code are Emmy, Dawson, and me."

"Your siblings?"

"Yes."

Stopping at the edge of the house, he pushed the garage door button built into his truck, and they waited silently for the door to open. She had plenty to take in as they waited. The scenery from up here was fabulous. Wild flowers dotted the area here and there where the trees parted and allowed the sun to shine through. Most of the remainder of the terrain was rocky but serene. They pulled into the garage, and the first thing she noticed was it was finished off and decorated in a country motif. Large eight-by-eight beams served as headers for the doors and windows. The doors were vertical barn boards with crossbeams creating an "X" in the middle of each. The whole garage looked heavily built and sturdy.

"Come on in and welcome to my home."

"I thought you said it wasn't yours or it was empty or something."

"Yeah. It's a long story."

"Well, it appears we'll have the time."

Ford lifted the tonneau cover of his truck and pulled her bag and purse from the back. He handed them to her as he walked past, pulling keys from his pocket. Inserting a key into the door, she watched as it swung open and the inside revealed itself to her.

Stepping into the kitchen, the same eight-by-eight header beams were evident as well as the barnwood doors. White cabinets graced three walls, and the dark granite countertops gleamed. The light fixtures all looked like old Mason jars, and rusty frames and shades held them in place. The pendant lights above the center island looked to be an old hay trolley with the same Mason jar lanterns suspended from it. Across from the island was a floor-to-ceiling fireplace of stacked stone in earth tones, and the same wooden beam as the headers served as a mantle. Completely unique and so incredible.

"Wow. This is amazing."

Looking to Ford, she saw the pride on his face. That same peaceful smile formed on his lips. "Thank you. The wood for the headers, mantle, and doors came from my father's barn. He helped me build this place. It was the last thing we did together."

He sucked in a deep breath and her heart hammered in her chest. "You have this beautiful home to remember him.

Did you enjoy the process of building this house with your dad?"

Nodding, he stood at the French doors and looked out onto the side of the mountain. "It was very special. As a kid, Dad could always fix everything, but building this home, I realized just how incredible his talent was." Turning to face her, he finished, "I learned so much from him."

Watching his face soften and then sadden broke her heart. She knew what it felt like to know you'd never see the people you loved anymore. It hurt.

"He left you with the most special gift. He taught you how to do something for yourself. Someday you'll be able to teach your children something their grandfather taught you."

His posture straightened. Clearing his throat, he said, "Um, yeah, well, anyway, your bedroom is over here." He walked toward a room off the living room/kitchen, the open concept intriguing and homey. The dark hardwood floors gleamed, the light tan walls soothing. The huge cream colored large pile area rug in front of the fireplace made her want to lay down and burrow in.

"You'll have your own bathroom just outside your door here." Reaching in, he flipped a light switch, and a classy bathroom with cream colored walls, a half bourbon barrel pedestal for the sink and the glass block enclosed shower greeted her. The copper fixtures and tile in the shower blended to create a sense of arms wrapping her in warmth. Whoever decorated this home knew what they were doing.

"It's beautiful."

Redness tinted his cheeks, but he smiled softly and locked gazes with her. When did those deep black pools begin to look sexy to her? Swallowing, he ducked out of the bathroom and stepped into the room next door. "This is your room. I hope you'll feel safe and comfortable here."

Stepping into the room, the dusty sage comforter and matching pillows called to her. When was the last time she'd slept? Three or four days now, if she were counting. Walking to the windows across from the bedroom, she marveled at the view she'd see when she'd wake in the morning. Mountains were in the distance, dotted with colorful flowers and green trees. How long did it take a person to tire or get used to this view? The blue of the sky was the crispest blue and set off the colors of the ground scenery perfectly. Turning, she saw a large wooden dresser, the drawers decorated with wrought iron handles.

"My father made that dresser and the bed. He also made the dresser and bed in my room."

She turned to look at the headboard on the bed; it was an old wooden door with wrought iron accents. "He was very talented."

Swallowing in rapid succession, she watched as he composed himself before saying anything. He simply turned and stepped from the room.

Following him out and deciding to change the subject, she asked, "Where may I do a little laundry? I'd like to get the smoky smell from my clothing, so I don't stink up the house."

"It's in the basement. Follow me." She followed him to the staircase just off the living room, down the steps, and into a finished lower level decorated the same as the upstairs. Opening the door to the left, they stepped into the laundry room, which was more than she expected. Front load washer and dryer sat on wooden pedestals with cabinets that matched the kitchen. A folding area stood along one wall with cabinets underneath.

"Help yourself to whatever you need. The laundry soap and fabric softener are under there." He pointed to one of the cabinets. "I'll get us something to eat for lunch while you situate yourself."

"You don't have to do that, Ford. I don't want—"

"We have to eat, and you need to start your laundry. It's fine." He turned to leave, and her heart thumped in her chest almost painfully. He was a kind man. Sad. Strong. Sexy. Everything a lucky woman could want. This was going to be hard staying here with him and not getting too close.

CHAPTER 12

Rummaging through the cupboards to find something to scrounge up for dinner, he tried relaxing his jaw. If he kept it clamped tightly like he was doing now, he'd end up with lockjaw or arthritis or something equally awful. But he was irritated that he was here in this house; he'd sworn he wouldn't come back until it was his completely—lock, stock, and barrel. The trouble was, when he tried to think of a safe place to keep Megan, this was the first place that came to mind. He knew it was safe; he'd built it with safety in mind. In his line of work, it wasn't uncommon for some of the people he had to locate to have angry family members or associates, and he didn't want to be taken unawares. Which reminded him—walking to the desk in the corner of the living room, he unlocked the top drawer. Lifting the lid on the laptop he kept in there, he waited for it to wake up, logged in, and pulled up his security system. Turning all the cameras on and monitoring the entire property via closed circuit monitors, he went back to the kitchen to finish looking for something to eat. Tomorrow he'd have to see if Emmy could bring some food up here.

A few cans of soup, some crackers, and some cans of peaches would be lunch—pretty bleak. Maybe he'd call Emmy to bring supper up. Turning, he spied the wine rack. Aah, things were looking up. Selecting a nice, full bodied red sangria, he set it on the counter as he pulled a pan from the drawer below the stove to heat the soup in. Setting to the task of pulling bowls and spoons from their respective spaces, he set their eating places at the counter. Wiping the dust from the wineglasses, he set them in front of the bowls and opened the shallow drawer that held the wine opener.

Popping the cork from the top, Megan entered the kitchen, a soft smile on her face. "How long have you lived here?"

"About eleven years."

She walked to the French doors and looked out over the scenery. "But you don't live here now?"

"No."

"Why?"

"It's a long story." He poured their glasses of wine. "It's also temporary."

She turned toward him, crossed her arms over her chest and stared at him. "Where do you live since you're not living here?"

He took a deep breath. Figures she'd want to know all about him. He didn't usually share much of his life. Still too much up in the air.

"I have a little cottage down the mountain by my sister's house. I stay there when I'm not working."

He watched her move toward him. The sun streaming through the French doors perfectly outlined her body in those sexy jeans and pink T-shirt. Purely sexy from head to toe. He'd bet she didn't even know it. Her full breasts jiggled as she walked, and his mouth went dry. It'd been far too long. Unfortunately, he hadn't thought this through completely. Staying here with her just might be harder than he thought.

"So, you work so much you have a house in the mountains you don't want to live in because it's a long story, so you stay in the cabin down by your sister. And then you go to work. Is that about right?"

"About."

She chuckled. "Well, I don't know how I'm going to get any peace here what with you talking so much and all."

Turning to the stove, he stirred the soup, twisted the knob on the stove to turn the burner off and filled both of their bowls.

"Vegetable soup and crackers and wine. It's not much, but it's all I have. I'll call Emmy to bring up some food later. I also have some meat in the freezer downstairs that I can thaw if Emmy's busy."

He sat next to her at the counter, and they began eating in silence. Or so he thought.

"What does Emmy do for a living?"

"She's a defense attorney. A damn good one too."

"Is your whole family involved with criminals?"

He chuckled. "Nah, just Emmy and me. Dawson's a plumber and owns his own company. He deals in shit, just not the same kind as Emmy and me."

She giggled. "That's a good one."

"So, tell me about Waylon. Why did you marry a piece of scum like him to begin with?"

She bit into a cracker and stared straight ahead. "Gosh damn, but isn't that the million-dollar question right now? I've been kicking myself since the first year."

She sipped her wine, and he watched her swallow, the graceful curve of her neck, her unblemished skin, her auburn hair looked thick and shiny, and he wanted to touch it—run his fingers through its softness and tuck the strands that had escaped her ponytail behind her delicate ear.

"In high school, he followed me around like a sad puppy. No matter where I went, he found me. After a while, I started talking to him, and he seemed nice enough. We became friends—just hanging out and watching television. I helped him with his homework and found him bright and eager to learn. He seemed ambitious, and I thought he'd really make something of himself. I went off to college in Kentucky for nursing, and he stayed in touch. When I came home to work at Kane County Hospital, he asked me out. It's not like I had a ton of other prospects, so I went out with him. We talked about his dreams for the future. He said he was working with a guy he liked and that he felt he'd be moving up in the company and was excited about it."

"What did he do?" Leaning back with his glass of wine, he watched her lips as she spoke.

"He said he was in transportation. Moving product." She sipped her wine again, then turned her head. "I was too stupid to ask what kind of product he moved. It took me years to figure it out." She shook her head, her lips turned into a frown.

"So, he was good at hiding it?"

"No, not really. I was just too absorbed in my own head to see it. By then my grandma had gotten sick and had to go to the nursing home. I changed jobs from Kane County to the nursing home, so I could watch over her. I spent a lot of time with her and Waylon worked weird hours and didn't demand a lot of my time. I actually thought it was nice. I could stay after work and sit with Grandma and not worry about having to be home at exactly five o'clock or something." She chuckled and shook her head.

"But, what happened then?"

She finished her glass of wine, and he reached forward to pour her another. He topped off his glass and sat back in his chair. He liked her voice. Not high-pitched and irritating, and when she chuckled, it was throaty and sexy.

"Oh, well, Grandma passed, and I was home more, and I began noticing things. Things came to a head when Waylon asked me to drop off a box for him at an associate's house in town. I should have asked what was in it, but I was still pretending I hadn't married a man who was capable of doing something illegal. I got caught up in a sting. The box contained money, and it appeared that I was a courier. I was arrested, thrown in jail for a couple of days until my sister could get me out, and then I divorced Waylon."

He stared into her eyes, telling himself not to get lost in them. "So, he was running drugs; that was the product he was transporting?"

"Yep, pretty stupid of me not to see it, right?"

"I wouldn't say that. It's amazing what we don't see when it's right there under our noses."

He jumped up to clear the dishes, but she followed him around the counter with her bowl in her hand. "I can clean up; you cooked."

"You're a guest. My mom would kick my ass if she thought I was making a guest work."

She giggled and shook her head. "Funny what sticks with us, isn't it?"

When she tilted her head up to smile at him, his gut twisted. He swallowed to moisten his instantly dried up throat and clenched his jaw—arthritis be damned. He inhaled deeply to get control of his breathing but what he smelled was her fresh, clean scent. Bad move.

Her face softened as she held his gaze, her head tipped

slightly to the left, which allowed him the perfect position to just lean forward and ... his lips touched hers, lightly at first but he felt her moan, the light rumble vibrating between them. Then her hand gently lay against his cheek. He deepened the kiss, his tongue sliding in at her invitation and the heady taste of wine and feel of her slippery tongue as it slid along his, exploring and tasting her fully made his head spin. Her hand fisted into his shirt, and his arms pulled her into his body. The instant her soft breasts flattened against his chest, his body came to life.

He pulled away gently and laid his forehead against hers until he could catch his breath. His heartbeat sounded loud in his ears, and he wondered if she could hear it too. Then she stepped back, and he could see her nipples through the pink T-shirt she wore. He'd need a code word for himself to drag his mind from her, her body, her being, and dampen any desire he was feeling. Tamra. He'd think of his wife; that would do it.

CHAPTER 13

Holy hell! She was bewildered that kissing could feel like that. Had her body ever responded to Waylon that way? The answer was a resounding no. Her heart was beating so hard she thought she'd pass out. Earth moving was an apt description. Her nipples beaded up, and the instant wetness between her legs sent a whole riot of emotions running through her. When he pulled her into his firm muscular body, her knees shook so badly she had to grip his shirt to keep from falling. Then he pulled away, and she wanted to cry at the loss.

Taking a deep breath, she stepped back again. "I should check on my laundry."

She saw him clench his jaw before she turned quickly and escaped to the basement, her face on fire. Switching her wet clothing to the dryer and hanging her wet bras on a hanger to dry, she tried focusing on what she was doing, but her head kept going back to the man upstairs who honestly seemed too good to be true. He was responsible, held a job, though it was terribly dangerous, and he was so very easy on the eyes. He thought nothing of bringing her here, a complete stranger, to keep her safe. He was nothing like Waylon.

Then her thoughts floated to that useless sack of human skin, Waylon. Besides working at all things illegal and wanting to get ahead in an organization that would always put them in danger, he'd gotten her arrested—on purpose. She'd found out after her arrest that he had gotten information that there was possibly something going down, and he felt that keeping her unaware ensured her release from jail because she'd have no information to release to authorities. She could still feel the anger of finding out he'd cared more for his stupid damned job than her. But in all honesty, hadn't she always cared more for hers and her grandmother than him? They'd been more roommates than lovers or husband and wife. Each living a separate life from the other. Thinking about it now made her sad and mad for the lost time in her life.

"You look lost in thought."

She jumped at the sound of his voice and being caught in her thoughts. Heat raged up her body and landed on her cheeks and ears as she turned to stare into the deep dark depths of his eyes. Damn, it would be so easy to look into his eyes forever. But that couldn't happen.

"Yeah, I guess I was." She glanced at her bras hanging in plain sight, and her cheeks burned hotter. She walked across the room where the counter for folding clothes stood, to bring his attention away from her hanging undergarments. "Um, did you need something?"

His lips turned up at the corners. "No, I just came down to pull something from the freezer for supper. Emmy can't come up tonight, but she'll bring groceries tomorrow. We'll have meat and scrounge up something else for the sides."

Stepping back, he stopped. "Please tell me you aren't a vegetarian."

Laughing, she shook her head. "No, I'm a carnivore. It's all good."

Nodding, he stepped from the doorway and disappeared. She couldn't stop herself from watching him walk down the hall. His ass was perfectly shaped and wore his jeans well. Firm round cheeks flowed into muscular legs. There was something about a man's well shaped thighs that had always been a turn on to her. His biker boots finished his attire, and she thought he'd look good no matter what he wore—a tuxedo or jeans and a T-shirt. Hearing the freezer door close, she stepped back into the laundry room and busied herself with her wet garments. Twisting the knob on the dryer to start the tumbling of her clothing, she tossed her dark clothing into the washer to clean up the last of her smelly clothes. Hopefully, that smell would wash away. Boots on the floor drew her gaze to the doorway. His dark head appeared for only a second as he held up a frozen roast, a captivating smile on his lips. "Roast beef for dinner; we won't starve."

Without waiting for a reply, he continued on upstairs, and she imagined what that would look like. Sucking in a deep breath, she pushed herself away from the counter and made her way upstairs. Her stomach rolled and tightened, but there were worse things than spending time with a handsome, yet sometimes scary man.

At the top of the stairs, she saw him sitting at a desk, his back slightly turned toward her, a computer up on the desk and a phone in his hand.

"I'm aware, Rory. I just need to make sure Megan's feeling secure here before ..."

She froze, and he turned toward her. Their eyes locked,

and he sat forward in his chair. As he stood, she turned abruptly and went into the room he'd allowed her to stay in. Her heart oddly hurt a bit at the implication that he might —what? Be using her to find Waylon? That's what she thought right now. Make sure she's feeling secure before he started grilling her with questions? Or, what else?

Furiously blinking away the tears, she walked to the window and looked out at the picturesque mountains and the vast array of colors that greeted her. Purples and yellows in the flowers that grew on the stony surface and the deep greens in the trees contrasted and brightened the blue hue of the sky to almost blindingly bright.

"Hey."

She spun around at the sound of his voice, so deep and sexy. But when she looked at him, she saw a puzzled look on his face. His brows were furrowed, and his lips turned slightly down.

"Are you okay?"

"Yes." Her tone wasn't clipped, but it was curt.

"You sure? Seems as though something's wrong."

"Why do I need to feel secure?"

He crossed his arms which made the muscles in his biceps bulge, and the effect was totally awesome. Dammit. He leaned against the doorframe and tried to look casual— he was anything but. His spine was rigid, and she'd learned that when he was trying to control himself, he clenched his jaw, which he was doing right now.

"Don't you want to feel secure?"

Planting her hands on her hips, she replied, "Of course I do. Who doesn't? But, why specifically do I before ... whatever you were going to say? I don't know where Waylon is. I haven't in years. Why don't you believe me?"

"For the record ..." He paused, and it made her nervous.

64

His dark eyes bored into hers, and with his jaw tight, he looked like scary Ford again. "I would like to make sure you feel secure here before I leave and go find Bobby Ray. In case you've forgotten, the murderer of my parents and your ex-husband are out there on the loose and committing crimes. Rather than being worried about whether or not you know where Waylon is, why don't you start thinking about someone else? Did it ever cross your mind that helping us find him and maybe Bobby Ray may help keep a lot of other innocent people safe?" He pushed himself from the door-jamb with a jerk of his shoulder. Hands at his sides, he turned to walk out the door but paused for a moment before adding, "I get you've had a rough week. But you aren't the only one."

And all she saw was his retreating back. The instant he left the room, she felt bereft and horrible. Had she been only thinking of herself? The argument could be and had been made to that effect. She'd lost her house, but she didn't lose her parents. Not like he had, anyway.

Hearing the back door open and close, she stepped from the safety of the bedroom and glanced out the kitchen window. Ford practically stomped out to the garage behind the house, opened the door, and disappeared inside. Her heart felt heavy, and she was ashamed of herself. Hearing the buzzer on the dryer go off, she went to the basement and pulled her dried clothing from the dryer and hung them on the hangers on a clothes rod between the cabinets—hopefully camouflaging her bras from his sight until they dried. How mortifying that had been.

Deciding she needed to be more appreciative, she made her way upstairs and scrounged around in the cupboards and refrigerator to see if she could find something to make for supper to go with their roast. She found a box of pasta and olive oil, and upon inspection of the cabinets, she found spices and enough ingredients to make a pesto. It wouldn't have the flavor of pesto with fresh herbs, but it would be something. Finding a box of Jell-O, she made them dessert to go with the rest. Pulling together her pesto and Jell-O, she placed the individual glasses filled with Jell-O in the refrigerator to firm up and set to the task of making the roast. Seasoning and placing it in the oven, she felt like she was contributing instead of just taking. It felt good.

———

Setting the smaller dining table alongside the counter, opposite the room from Ford's desk, she arranged the plates and silverware. Wineglasses sat before the plates, and a bottle of red sat in the middle of the table—opened and breathing before dinner.

Her stomach flipped when she heard the back door open and close, and Ford's footsteps coming toward her. She turned and caught his eyes with hers as he rounded the corner to the kitchen.

"It smells amazing in here. I was just coming in to make supper, but it looks as though you have it covered."

"Thank you. I hope you don't mind that I rummaged around. I found some things that I hope will be suitable for a side and a dessert. The roast should be ready in about ten minutes, so your timing is great."

"I'll just go shower up quickly then." He continued across the living room and to a doorway that she'd looked at but was afraid to peek into for fear she'd feel too nosy.

Emptying the pasta from the pot, she poured the pesto over it and tossed it in the pan. Pulling the roast from the oven, she had to admit, everything smelled fantastic. She sliced the meat and arranged it on a plate and set it on the table. Ford sauntered in, hair still wet and gleaming, his black Harley shirt clinging in the spots he'd dried fleetingly and left damp. Wearing his customary blue jeans, she smiled that he always seemed ready for anything but so very handsome.

"Smells great."

"Thanks."

She sat as he poured their wine. Smiling as he eagerly dug into the roast, the tightness in her stomach eased.

"I'm sorry about earlier, Ford. I guess I was having a very long pity party for myself, and I apologize."

"I understand. It's over, let's move forward."

Nodding, she twirled her fragrant pasta on her fork and scooped it into her mouth. Not bad for a thrown together dish. "Why don't you live here? This is an amazing kitchen with the most outstanding view. Plus, all of the special wood and memories of your dad. I don't understand."

Swallowing his food, he sipped at his wine. "I have to settle some personal things before I can live here again. But, it'll happen."

"I hope so. I mean, I hope so for you." They finished their meal while chatting about the mountains, his parents, and his siblings. She told him about her sister, Delaney, and brother, Cord. It was nice.

"Let's take our wine into the living room and sit in front of the fire. It'll start getting chilly in a little while. As soon as the sun begins setting, the weather changes here."

He leaned before the fireplace and expertly started a fire, which she had to admit was impressive. Watching the muscles in his back strain and stretch as he moved was exciting. She tightened her thighs to stem the wetness as she watched him. Waylon never had this effect on her, and it was mystifying.

He moved to sit on the sofa next to her—it was cozy. The only light in the room was from the fire and the light above the stove; the soft glow and glasses of wine made her tummy feel funny. Relaxing for the first time in weeks, she let out a sigh.

"It's nice, isn't it?"

"It sure is." She laid her head back on the sofa, and her eyes drifted closed. The next thing she knew, she felt like she was floating on a cloud. With leather and wood scent of man and firm arms around her, she'd never felt so safe in her life. She lived in the mountains with a view so beautiful, it could make a stone cry. She felt loved in a way she'd never felt in all her forty-two years. The loneliness of her life peeled away, and she knew what life could be like.

CHAPTER 14

He had to admit she was a beauty. Thick auburn hair and those eyes of green reminded him of a fresh spring morning. So fresh and full of promise. She felt light as a feather as he carried her to the bedroom he'd had his sister decorate for him. He'd scoffed when she came up with the dusty sage color, but he had to admit, it worked.

Laying Megan on the bed, he bent down to remove her shoes. A little moan escaped her lips, and he looked up to see her eyes on him. "Sorry, I guess I fell asleep."

"That's okay. It's been a long few days, and I'll bet you didn't sleep much the last couple of nights."

She chuckled. "No."

He set her shoes on the floor next to the bed but stopped and stared into her eyes. Her hair fanned across the pillow and the green of her eyes blended with the sage of the comforter. Totally beautiful.

Without thought, he leaned down and kissed her lips lightly—thinking just a little peck would be enough to hold him over. Since he'd kissed her earlier, he'd replayed that kiss in his mind a million times. Her lips were soft and molded to his perfectly. When her breasts pressed against his chest, he tried remembering a time when a woman felt that good against him, but he couldn't recall such a feeling.

Pulling back so he didn't get carried away, he was shocked when her hand wrapped around his nape and pulled him down for another kiss. Fuller and bolder this time, his body responded. He cupped her face between his hands as he tilted her head slightly to fit his lips perfectly to hers. His tongue slid along hers, and when she whimpered, his heart raced.

His fingers itched to touch her body, feel her soft breasts fill his hands, and without thought, he slid a hand down to cup her. Just as he thought, she filled his hand as if she were made just for him. Her soft hands sifted through his hair, her nails lightly scratching his scalp. It sent a shiver down his body, and his breathing grew stilted.

Pulling back, he lay his forehead against hers.

"Wow," she whispered, and he had to agree.

"I better let you get some rest. You have to deal with my sister tomorrow. She's a force all on her own." Smiling to add levity, he stood to his full height, but her hand caught his.

"Thank you for making sure I'm safe. I haven't said it, but I do appreciate it." A soft smile spread across her lips, and his heart practically stopped at the sight of her.

"You're welcome." His voice cracked; he cleared his throat and took a step back. Better to have some distance. But the second her hand fell away, he felt lonely. "Sleep well, Megan."

Closing the bedroom door on his way out, he let out a deep breath. Picking up the fire poker, he jabbed a few times at the logs still emitting a soft glow. Sparks flew up the chimney, and he watched them rise until he couldn't see them anymore. He was in over his head here. Somewhere along the way, she ceased to be a woman who needed help and became a woman he was deeply attracted to and wanted. When he'd walked in from the garage after having his pity party, the smell of a freshly cooked meal and her standing in his kitchen hit him hard. It was the sight he'd always longed for in this house. At one time, he thought that person would be Tamra, but she turned out to be someone different from what he'd thought. She'd hated this house, hated living here, hated him, hated everything, including their son, even though she pretended to care about Falcon when it was convenient.

Megan was embroiled in some shit that he didn't even know the extent of, and on top of that, the drugs. He had no inkling that she used or ever had used, but she had a connection, and he wanted nothing to do with that.

He'd try and get a good night's rest and deal with digging in to where Bobby Ray and Waylon were in the morning. Turning toward his computer on the desk in the corner, he checked the security system, then quickly browsed his emails. Nothing of huge importance about his case, but a quick note from Falcon.

Dad, things have been quiet here most of the day. We assume the insurgents are planning something, but we're ready. We sent out more balloons this morning and found a few of them in the pot fields. Other than that, hope all is well with you. Aunt Emmy sent me a giant box of cookies, which I'll admit didn't make it very long. My buddies and I devoured them. She should have opened a bakery.

Anyway, I'll call when I can, but in the meantime, I love you, and things are quiet here in Kandahar.

Falcon

Staring at the monitor, several emotions flooded his

body. Pride. He was so proud of his son. He'd grown to be a fabulous man. He'd moved up the ranks in the Army quickly because of his work ethic. He'd instilled that in him from the beginning. Falcon's rank was already the same grade as his own at E7. But Falcon had already told his dad he was staying in. He loved it in the Army.

Clicking on reply, he penned an email to his son.

It's so good to hear from you, and I'm glad things are quiet. Don't let your guard down. Emmy will be thrilled to hear you devoured her cookies; that's why she sent them. I'm sure there will be more coming as soon as she hears how much you love them.

Things are quiet here. I'm back at the house for a while and more determined than ever to find a way to stay here permanently. I miss you and wish you were here. Do you have a return date to the states?

Keep your head down.

Love, Dad

Closing his eyes, he sent up a silent prayer for Falcon's safe return. Another for himself. He would need it to keep his head about him and accomplish all he needed to. Things were getting complicated.

CHAPTER 15

Waking with the sun streaming in through the windows, she sat up in the bed and marveled at this view. For as far as she could see, the mountains greeted her with greens and flowers, and white caps had been added overnight. It was stunning. Wrapping her arms around her bent knees, she rested her chin on them and allowed her thoughts to float to Ford.

How could he be happier in a cabin at the bottom of the mountain than up here with this view? This house held so much meaning for him. From the wood used to build it to the memories of his father building it with him. It made no sense that he had something to "work out." But, it really wasn't her business, so she'd only hope he'd share if he wanted, and if not, he wasn't the man she thought he was. It would help her keep her emotions in check cause she'd never be with a man again who kept secrets from her. Not again. Not ever.

Throwing the covers aside, she left her warm, comfy bed and rummaged in the dresser for her clothes. Stepping quietly to the door, she listened to see if he was in the kitchen. Her bedroom was across the house from his, but he had a straight view from the kitchen area to the bathroom door, and she didn't want him to see her until she showered and added a little bit of makeup. She'd figure out what to do with her hair after she saw what it did in this humidity.

Silence greeted her, so she cracked the door, peeked out, didn't see Ford, and skittered quickly to the adjacent door. Twisting the handle to start the shower warming, she again marveled at the beauty of this house. The earth toned tile work in the bathroom was something of a professional designer's touch. Perfectly matched border tiles and copper fixtures set the room's tone to natural, from the earth, but also pleasing to the eye. Undressing and stepping under the warm stream of water, a wild shiver raced down her body. A little bit of heaven after all she'd been through.

After showering and drying her hair, the humidity won and the curls she tried so hard to hide made their appearance. She didn't have a flat iron here, so she'd need to resort to ponytails to tame the wild mess. Pulling it high up on her head, she wrapped it around in a messy bun, donned some mascara and lip gloss and heaved out a big sigh. She was nervous to see him this morning, though she didn't know why. Probably because she'd kissed him back last night. Being honest, she wanted to do more than that. He was simply the most handsome man she'd ever met. His quiet reserve was comforting to be around. Then there was the commitment to his family and the way his voice changed when he spoke of his father. It softened and lowered. His face took on a serene quality when he spoke of his parents. And, when he talked about Emmy, it was as if he couldn't stop the soft smile that widened his full, sensual lips. This man cared. She couldn't recall being around a man who cared for the people in his life.

Hesitating a moment, she lay her hand on her stomach to quell the rolling. "Here goes," she whispered as she pulled the door open. Scooping up her pajamas, she scurried to the bedroom and lay the folded night clothes at the foot of the bed. The aroma of coffee wafted in and her mouth watered. Her favorite thing in the morning was the smell of coffee.

Softly walking into the open area that served as the living room and kitchen, her heartbeat sped up. He stood at the stove, scrambling eggs. The tight Army green T-shirt he wore stretched across his shoulders. It molded to his body like a glove, and for the first time, she could actually see the muscular frame beneath. The green hugged his frame like a lover, narrowed at his waist, and disappeared into the softly faded jeans. Just like the pants he wore yesterday, these hugged his perfectly shaped ass and strong thighs, revealing the incredible shape he was in. A soldier still. Her head turned to the array of pictures on the fireplace mantle and the photographs of a younger Ford in his uniform. The smile on his handsome face was breathtaking. Another with him and men alongside and kneeling in front of him, dirt smudged on their faces and a desert behind them. Counting out the years, she guessed this was the Desert Storm conflict, and he was there. She wanted to ask last night but lost her nerve. Some soldiers didn't like talking about the conflict they'd seen.

"That's my crew in Iraq. We were there for a year before coming home." He took a deep breath, and his voice cracked. "Not all of us came home."

He walked across the room to the fireplace, and as if a rope tied them together, she followed. As she stood next to him, she realized just how tall he was—at least a foot taller than her. Raising his arm, he pointed to the men in the picture. "Seth died a week after this picture was taken."

Moving to the man to his right, he said, "Smith did as well." Moving past himself, he pointed to the man on his left. "Jackson came home with one arm. The next in line ... Rory is my best friend and the Chief Detective in Lynyrd Station." The two men kneeling in front of him in the picture is where his finger went next. "Lincoln and Dodge both came home when Rory, Jackson, and I did." A softness washed over his face as his eyes searched the faces in the picture, but she'd stopped looking at the men and watched Ford. "This picture was taken after we were engaged in battle just outside of Baghdad. We defeated the enemy that day with no casualties. It was always a reason to celebrate when that happened. We didn't have alcohol there, so we celebrated with a glass of milk from the mess tent and candy bars we bought from the Iraqi traders that wandered the dessert."

He moved on to other pictures on the mantle, and she was torn between watching him and looking at the pictures. Her heart flipped and beat an irregular rhythm as she gazed at his profile. Strong firm jaw, not clenched in frustration or control, but softened in what she'd describe as love. She wondered what it would feel like for him to look at her that way. She gently shook her head to turn her thoughts away from that train of thought. Didn't she just tell herself to keep her feelings at bay?

"This is Emmy and her family. Her husband, Scott, and Dillon and Raye Anne." He moved on to the picture alongside. "This is my brother, Dawson. His wife Sylvia, and their kids, David, Jessica, Matthew, and Mark."

Moving to the larger portrait of an older couple, the man's dark head and eyes identical to Ford's, she knew without a doubt that these were his parents. "My parents, Ray and Darlene Montgomery. The finest people to ever walk the earth."

Sadness washed over his beautiful face, and her heart hurt for him. Without thought, she wrapped her arms around his waist and squeezed him to her. Pressing her cheek to his chest, she let his scent seep into her. Leather and wood and man. Her eyes closed as she listened to his strong heartbeat against her face and as his arms wrapped around her in return, she heard his heartbeat speed up.

When she felt him lay his cheek on the top of her head and heard him inhale her scent, she squeezed her eyes shut tighter, and her body shook with a riot of emotions she struggled to understand.

His arms tightened around her shoulders, pulling her tighter to him, flattening her body to his, their hearts beat together in a steady rhythm she didn't recognize but knew it was pure. She lifted her head and felt bad when he stood taller, removing his cheek from her head. Lifting her right hand, she cupped his jaw, gently running her thumb over his freshly shaven cheek. His dark, shiny eyes bored into hers, and her breathing tumbled from her lungs in short bursts. His head began to lower, but he stopped, never breaking eye contact with her. Softly smiling and praying he'd kiss her, it was as if he could read her mind. When his lips touched hers, the excitement that raced through her body was difficult to contain.

Pliant, soft lips enveloped hers and instantly commanded her mouth. His delicious tongue, tasting of fresh coffee and warm against hers danced in her mouth—touching, tasting, and exploring every surface. A moan—more like a whimper—escaped her throat and a groan from him. His breathing grew stilted, and she realized that she had the same effect on him as he had on her. It was exhilarating and exciting, and her heart opened to something new and delicious even though it was scary. Her experience with men was limited to Waylon, and her body never responded to him as it did to Ford. She suddenly felt stupid and naïve and out of her league. Ford probably had women all over the world panting for his attention. But, more than ever, she wanted to learn, feel, explore, and be wanted as a woman. Desirable and beautiful and worthy of a man like this man right here in her arms.

"Okay, someone come and help me carry in groceries."

She jumped back as a woman's voice carried in from the garage door.

A handsome smile appeared on his face. "That's Emmy. Hang on."

He turned toward the garage, and she admired his retreating backside a moment before following him to help.

Reaching the door that separated the house from the garage, what she saw was Ford hugging a woman about her height with his same dark hair tight to him. When they separated, he glanced at her and motioned with his hand for her to join them.

"Megan, this is Emmy, my sister. Emmy, Megan."

"Nice to meet you, Megan. Has my crabby brother been giving it to you?"

Her cheeks flamed so brightly she could feel it in her ears. "Um ..."

Emmy cocked her head just a bit and burst out laughing. "Well, now I really need to know what's been going on." Stepping closer to her, Emmy continued, "I meant giving you grief. He can be a real sorry soul sometimes, but the bright red of your cheeks tells me you two have been involved in much more."

"Um. I ..."

"Leave her alone, Em." He turned his dark gaze to her, a bit of mirth in his expression. "I told you she was a force."

"Well, now that we've got that out of the way, here you go." She handed grocery bags to both of them and grabbed two herself and headed into the house. Ford closed the tailgate of her SUV and smiled at her as he followed his sister into the house.

Her panties dampened with just his smile. To say "Oh. My. Gawd." would be an understatement. His kind smile was breathtaking. He probably didn't even realize what a picture he made.

Numbly following them into the house with the groceries, she worked to focus on not tripping—on her words or her feet. All this before her first cup of coffee; it was going to be a long day.

CHAPTER 16

He'd need to keep his distance. That's what he knew right now. Three times he'd kissed her, and each time, his feelings became jumbled into a mash of something he couldn't describe. First of all, his life was a mess on its own. Secondly, he had to leave here—and soon—to find Bobby Ray, if for no other reason than one of the women standing in his kitchen right this minute. Emmy. She and Dawson trusted him to bring Bobby Ray to trial, and he'd do just that. His parents deserved that. And third, Tamra. He still had that wreckage to clean up, but he was more determined than ever to extricate her from his life. Bringing another woman, even one as special as Megan, into that chaos, was crazy.

"So, tell me what the plan is?"

Emmy and Megan both looked at him, waiting for a response to Emmy's question.

Taking a deep breath, he responded, "I want to get Megan secured up here where she won't be found by Marcus and his happy henchmen, then I'm going back down to South Point to bring in Bobby Ray."

"Okay, good." Emmy took charge, always, which is what made her a damn good attorney, but sometimes she could be over-bearing. His back stiffened as he recognized over-bearing Emmy coming out. He poured a cup of coffee for Megan and slid it across the counter to her, along with a sugar bowl and creamer pot. He glanced at his sister, who held up her neon green covered cup she almost always carried. Nodding, he warmed his own up with a topping of fresh coffee from the pot. He watched Megan smile when he slid her cup to her then slowly poured a dash of creamer from the pot into it. She drank her coffee just like he did, cream no sugar.

Her delicate fingers wrapped around the cup which seemed an effort to warm her fingers from the cup but maybe she was holding on to something in case Emmy began barking out orders for their lives.

"So, when will that be? Tomorrow, the next day? And what do you need Dawson and me to do?"

"Em, slow down." His eyes flicked to Megan, and his heart sped up when hers locked onto his. He'd just noticed that her hair was an auburn pile of curls on top of her head and it softened her features, almost making her look like a younger woman in her early twenties. He knew otherwise from Waylon's file, which stated she was forty-two. The soft column of her neck exposed how petite her bone structure was. The line of her collarbone made his fingers itch to touch her creamy skin. Those green eyes always seemed to stop him in his tracks. He'd tossed and turned last night remembering the way she looked laying on the bed in the other room, the way her eyes beaconed him to touch her, kiss her, fuck her. He'd seen it there, or maybe he'd imagined it because that's what he was thinking. But she was too vulnerable right now, and he didn't want to make that mistake again. The last time had been disturbing, to say the least.

"Well, it seems I may have interrupted something here this morning since you two can't stop making googly eyes at each other, so I'll just say this. You need to get rid of Tamra and get on with your life. You need to get this house out of her name and into yours only, and you need to bring peace to Mom and Dad. With that, I'm off to a soccer game this morning. Dillon is starting. I told him you couldn't make it because of work, but we're hoping you can make it next week."

Taking a breath and turning to Megan, his sister beamed at her. "Please join Ford at Dillon's soccer game next week. He's pretty good and he just loves his uncle."

Picking up her cup, she strode around the counter and hugged him tightly. "I used your bank card to buy the groceries. Change the password on the gate, please, it's been two weeks. See ya." And with an absent wave, she was out the door.

Turning to Megan, he was shocked at the change in her features. Tense wasn't a strong enough word, and the air seemed to crackle with anger and hostility.

"Who's Tamra?"

Clenching his jaw, he inhaled; the time was now. "My wife."

"Your wife? You're fucking married? You kissed me. Three times. In your wife's house. In the house you share with your wife?" Each 'your wife' was punctuated with a hint of disgust.

"It's not like that."

"It never is, is it? Men always say shit like that when they've been caught cheating."

"I didn't cheat."

"You thought about it."

Raising his voice, he nearly hollered. "You don't know what I've thought about. You don't know anything about me."

"That's because you don't share. Other than those pictures this morning and a bit about your siblings and parents, you conveniently left out any talk about a fucking wife."

She turned and stalked to the patio doors, turned back, and stalked toward him. He was immensely happy the granite counter separated them right now. "Am I even safe here or is there going to be a rabid wife walking through the door any moment? She could have walked in on us kissing. Wouldn't that have been grand? What would you have said, 'It's not like that?' You're no different than Waylon. Lying, cheating. Gah." She turned to stalk away again.

"Hey!" he yelled. Her head snapped, and she swung around. Waiting a moment to gather his thoughts, he swallowed and inhaled a cleansing breath.

"First of all, I'm nothing like that piece of shit you married. Second of all, while I may still be married, we haven't lived together for years. She's living in town with her boyfriend slash supplier."

Her head jerked back slightly, but her eyes were still narrowed when she looked at him. "Yes, supplier. Tamra has been a raging drug addict for years. She blew through our money, then began hitting her parents up for money until her father finally cut her off. So, she moved in with her supplier and I suppose she pays for her drugs with sex. Don't know. Don't care."

He slammed his hand on the unforgiving granite counter and winced as the sting flew up his arm.

Her voice softened. "Why didn't you divorce her?"

He looked her in the eye. He wanted her to know he was telling the truth. He saw them glisten with moisture, and her lips sucked into her mouth in an effort to stem the crying.

"I filed for divorce years ago. But when it came to dividing up our household, she refused to let me have the house. She wanted to hurt me. She knows this house means everything to me. I offered to buy her out, even willing to pay triple the value, but she said no. So, we stalled right where we're at. I moved out, mostly, to get my thoughts in order. I've put an awful lot of emotion into this house and especially after my parents died, thinking if I left for a while I'd realize it didn't mean as much to me as I thought, and she'd see it didn't mean that much and let it go. I was wrong. It means everything to me. She hates this place and everything about it, so I know it's just to twist the knife in my back. Then I got busy looking for Bobby Ray and was gone a lot, so I just let it ride, thinking eventually she'd want to remarry and then I'd have a bit of leverage."

"If her parents cut her off financially, why wouldn't she take the money?"

"Her boyfriend, Stephano, keeps her in constant supply. She doesn't need the money anymore." Swallowing the bile that rose in his throat, he glanced at the picture of his parents, his jaw tensing painfully tight.

"I've got some things to take care of in the garage," he managed to get out before the anger that was bubbling close to the surface boiled over. He stalked out the door to the garage, hit the opener and ducked under the opening door as soon as he could. He continued on to the garage out back, punishing the ground with every step to keep from hitting something.

CHAPTER 17

Married. He was still married?

It hit her hard in the gut. Tears trailed down her face and splashed onto her shirt. She'd gone and let herself begin to feel something for him, and he'd been lying to her. Or, according to him, just not sharing the whole truth. And, he was correct in that she didn't know a lot about him. It was just this stupid attraction. Then her heart softened when she saw his face change to that handsome, caring, loving man. But, she should know better. There'd never been a man in her life that was true to his word or caring. If they cared, they eventually left or screwed up in some damnable way and left her just the same. Her father, Waylon, even her brother. They all left.

Hurrying to her room, she dug through her purse and found her phone. She owed Jolie a call, but she'd still be getting kids ready for the day. She'd just send her a message and call in a bit. Holding the power button to turn it on, her mind raced, and her heart, well ... she was trying to keep it from breaking. Tapping her friend's number, she sent a quick text then watched as the phone tried to connect.

Nothing. That damn little circle just spinning while her phone tried connecting her to the world at large. Shit.

They'd both be better off if she just left. For some stupid reason, he wanted to help her, and she allowed it because she had nowhere to go and no one to help her. She'd just lost everything she ever owned, save for her Jeep, which was still locked in the garage wrapped in crime scene tape.

Ford managed to get calls up here, so she'd need his Wi-Fi password or figure out what was wrong with her phone. As soon as he came in, she'd get that and make arrangements to hop on a bus back to South Pass. Then, she'd figure something out, even if it meant calling her sister, Delaney. They'd have to talk eventually, and of course, she'd never hear the end of needing a favor from her. It would be miserable having to stay with her, but she was growing feelings for Ford, and she couldn't let that happen. Especially since he's married.

Sniffing away the new tears that sprang to the surface, she tossed her phone on the bed, pulled her bag from the closet, and began packing her clothing. She still had clothing hanging downstairs, so she softly walked to the basement steps and descended. Flipping the light switch, she entered the brightly lit laundry room, which she took in with new eyes. Ford and his father had built this entire house, including this room. The cabinets were painted white, but when she looked closer at the room, she saw the farmhouse sink on the opposite wall from the washer and dryer. The countertops were matching granite from the upstairs, and the tile floors looked like hardwoods. A picture hanging on the wall across from the folding counter caught her attention, and she stepped up to it to take a closer look. Three barn boards held together with two boards across the back, pushing it away from the wall a half inch. A sunflower in bright yellow and orange was painted in the middle of the barn boards, its bright green stem and leaves adding a bit more color. In the bottom right hand corner, it said D. Montgomery. Darlene—his mom. Even her touches were in this house, and she wondered if his mom helped to design some of the elements of the home.

Her chest felt heavy, her heart heavier. This home meant so much to him. He probably saw his parents on every surface, and she'd just bitched at him about it. Well, not the house but the fact he hadn't shared anything about his wife. And, honestly, who the hell was she to demand anything of him about his most personal life? She hadn't shared everything about herself either. She'd just hoped that he was beginning to feel things for her like she was feeling for him, and he'd want her to know about his life—all of his life. Isn't that what relationships were founded on? Learning about each other? Crap.

Setting about pulling her bras from the hanger and folding them on the counter, she heard a click. Freezing in mid fold, she listened again. Click. Her heartbeat raced so fast she thought she'd throw up. That was the same sound she'd heard just before her house caught on fire. They'd found her. Up here in the mountains. *Oh my God!*

Frantically, she ran from the room and down the hall she'd seen Ford walk down yesterday. There were other rooms and maybe a way out of the house from down here. The first room was a bedroom, decorated in red and blue military motif. Scrambling from that doorway, she ran to the next one and found the freezer he'd pulled their supper from, a furnace, water heater, and other equipment. She stopped and listened again, not hearing footsteps, but not brave enough to go upstairs. She swallowed the bile that rose in her throat and made her way to another room, which seemed bright with sunlight streaming in. It was a den with high bookshelves filled to the top with books of all kinds. An older, comfortable looking recliner sat next to a low table where a lamp sat on top and a book resting alongside with a bookmark protruding. The room felt totally different from any other room in the house and like a personal room, forbidden from the eyes of anyone else. The tall windows caught her eye, and she ran to them and looked out. This room was directly under the living room and looked out over the mountains. Trying the window, she found a latch and slid it open. Heaving herself over the sill, she didn't have far to drop before her bare feet hit the cool stones below. Not sure which direction to run, she slowly climbed up toward the back of the house, keeping herself low in case anyone was in the house and would see her and trying to keep her feet from being cut on the rocks. Once she made her way to the back of the house, she glanced at the back garage she'd seen Ford stalk off to and decided she could run to that garage and hide. She'd never be able to run down the stone driveway without shoes.

Making it to the side door of the garage, relief washed over her when she twisted the handle, and it opened. As slowly as she could, she stepped in and closed the door quietly behind her. The darkness in the room caused her to freeze to allow her eyes time to adjust. The cold cement bit into her bare feet and eerie silence greeted her. The odor of motor oil, dust, and leather greeted her nose. Shakily, she reached out to the wall, taking small steps forward, inching her way into the garage.

"Ford." Her shaky voice managed to whisper. Her hands and feet shook with fear.

As the garage slowly came into view, she could see an older Jeep parked in the back, sun from the windows streaming in, glinting off the Army green paint. Chipped and worn but oddly cared for. Alongside a cart held tools and small parts haphazardly strewn across the top. Ford isn't here, the lights are off. He must have gone for a hike or walk to clear his head. It was her own fault, she had no right to confront him.

Walking toward the Jeep, she scooted herself behind it and lowered her shaking body to the ground. Knees bent up, arms hugging them, she swallowed to push the large dry knot in her throat down. She'd just stay here for a bit until her heartbeat returned to normal. Nervousness didn't allow her to relax and constantly staying vigilant began grating on her psyche.

Wishing Ford was here right now, she squeezed her eyes closed and silently vowed that if she got out of this alive, she'd tell Ford why Marcus is after Waylon and help him figure out where to find him, and hopefully, Bobby Ray too. Admitting that he makes her feel safe didn't come as much of a shock as she would have thought.

Hearing footsteps nearing the door she'd just entered through, she stopped breathing. The clicking of the door handle sounded as loud as a bomb in the quiet room, but the erratic beating of her heart began to drown out all other sound. Biting her bottom lip to keep from whimpering, she shrank down farther, and the thought of rolling under the back of the Jeep entered her head, just as the door opened and someone stepped inside.

CHAPTER 18

Kicking around the garage for a few minutes, irritation and frustration gnawing at his gut, he begrudgingly admitted to himself that Megan was right. Or, partly right. Dammit, he should have told her about Tamra both times they'd chatted about his family. He was self-analyzing why he didn't come up with any answers—embarrassment, maybe? Hoping if things started up between them the answers he'd sought for the past five fucking years would magically appear to him in thin air, and he'd be able to finally rid himself of Tamra once and for all were completely and utterly stupid. Of course, it was easy to see now.

Walking to his old Jeep, actually his dad's old Jeep, he looked over all the tools and parts displayed on the cart, trying to remember where he'd left off on the repair work. Picking up a screw and some washers, he stared at them, wondering where to begin. His mind was usually quieted and focused once he got out here and worked on this old truck. But, not today. He knew stalking out and leaving never solved anything. Tucking the hardware into his pocket, he lovingly ran his hand over the softly worn leather of the driver's seat. He imagined his dad sitting there, his smile as wide as the barn, happy to be here in his beloved Jeep with his son, working together once again.

"Dad, what do I do now? She's got me tied up in knots."

His dark head turned, those deep black eyes so much like his own shined upon him, and his dad said back to him, "Go be the man I taught you to be. You screwed up. Admit it. Apologize for it. Move past it."

Swallowing the large knot in his throat, the moisture gathering in his eyes made the vision he'd imagined of his dad float away and disappear. A quick shake of his head and he knew his dad was right.

Walking quietly back to the house, he entered from the garage. Opening the back door to the house, he slipped into the back washroom to wash his hands and splash water on his face. Pulling his shaking right hand from his pocket, he dropped the screw and then one of the washers on the floor. Bending to retrieve them, he chastised himself for being clumsy and scolded himself to get a grip.

Once he'd washed and dried his hands and face, he silently walked into the kitchen. Disappointment caved in his chest when he found it empty. She looked good standing in his kitchen, smiling as she worked. Her very presence lit the room with a light from within. Crossing the floor to her bedroom, even though the door was open, he knocked and stuck his head in. "Megan?"

Greeted with silence, he tamped down the panic he'd begun to feel and checked that her bathroom was empty. As his heartbeat increased, he checked his bedroom, the mud room, and the deck off the living room patio doors. His phone sent off a double buzz, and he quickly pulled it from his back pocket. The security system alerting him that the window in the den downstairs had been opened. Rushing to the basement stairs, he descended as quietly as he could in case someone who isn't supposed to be here had entered the house. Pulling the gun from inside his waistband, he dropped his arm to his side and peered around the corner. Finding an empty hallway, he peered into each door as he advanced to the den.

Glancing around the doorway, what he's greeted with was an empty room and an open window. He managed to groan out "Megan" before rushing and looking out at the ground below. The rocky surface below the window doesn't leave footprints as dirt or sand would, and he quickly made a mental note to change the landscape around the house.

Running to the back door just the next room from the den, he exited the house and slowly made his way around the side and to the back of the house. No one was there. Nothing of note disturbed and no Megan.

Glancing at the back garage once again, he headed that way to make sure she hadn't come looking for him. Swallowing the panic that threatened and taking deep breaths to calm his ragged breathing, he spotted smears of blood on the stones. The thumping of his heart made his hands shake, the churning of his stomach now threatening to let loose the piece of toast he'd eaten this morning. Turning the handle on the garage door, he eased himself inside, closing the door silently and flattening his back against the wall. Allowing his eyes to adjust, he took in his surroundings. Keeping his footfalls quiet, he stepped farther into the garage. That's when he heard her. A soft whimper that was barely discernible, but loud enough in the quiet of the garage to be heard. Turning his head in the direction of her voice, he struggled to listen. Her breathing was coming in short spurts—similar to that of a scared child. Glancing at the floor, he saw more smears of blood and inhaled deeply at the thought she might be injured.

"Megan?" He called to her, still wary in case she wasn't alone. Her soft, shaky voice replied, "Ford?"

He walked past the Jeep to the back of the garage and saw her eyes, round and dark peering up at him from her crouched position, the fear evident in them and on the tightness in her usually serene face.

He whispered as his head swiveled around, "Are you alone?"

Her head bobbed quickly up and down.

In one swift move, he holstered his gun and bent to scoop her into his arms. He crushed her to his chest and wrapped his arms around her. Her arms quickly wrapped around his neck and she cried into the crook of his neck where it connected to his shoulder. Her heaving shaking body felt warm against his, her fresh scent floated to his nostrils, and he had to fight to control his rampant heartbeat.

He crooned soft reassuring words into her ear and hair. "You're safe. It's okay, honey. What happened? Why are you out here? It's okay. I'm here. I won't let anything happen to you, honey."

Between sobs, she managed a few words. "I thought they found me. I heard a noise." She tightened her arms around his neck and burrowed deeper into his body.

"Okay. Shush, it's okay, honey. You're safe." He felt like a heel using her fear to continue holding her, but dammit she felt perfect crushed against him. Her lush curves fitted themselves to his body as if she were made for him.

He held her tightly until he felt her shaking subside a bit, then he reluctantly pulled away to look at her.

"What did you hear?"

"Two clicks or taps or something." She swallowed, "It sounded just like before the fire at my house. Like something dropping or something, I don't know, then the flames started."

"Okay." Smoothing his fingers lightly over her soft cheeks, he said, "Honey, my house isn't on fire. I think that was me you heard. I came in the back door."

Her features held that puzzled look for just a couple of seconds, then her hands flew up to cover her face. "Oh, God, I feel so stupid."

He kissed the top of her head and breathed her in. Slowly her hands moved away from her face and wrapped around his shoulders.

"I'm sorry," she said into his neck. "I think we need to talk."

"I do too."

Then she kissed his neck, and he heard her inhale his scent followed by a soft moan. More kisses followed by a little nip just below his ear and his body roared to life. Blood thrumming through his veins made it hard to hear anything but her soft breathing, the sound of her kisses on his neck and her light little moans.

Holy fuck!

CHAPTER 19

Mmm. He smelled so good. He felt so perfect against her body. So right. She kissed his neck without thinking and the way she felt his body respond made it totally worth it. She made him feel like that. Like he made her feel. She felt the thickening of his cock behind that offensive zipper, but she felt how quickly it grew for her. She sighed with relief because she wasn't sure he felt the same way as she did. She felt right here, with him. As long as they were here, secluded up in the mountains, why couldn't they enjoy each other in a physical sense? They were both in their forties, unmarried ...

Nope, that's why. He was still married. She pulled away, "Maybe we can go back to the house and talk?"

"Sure."

She saw the confusion in the sudden change of mood. She didn't want to be a tease. Not only was that not nice, but she also didn't want to do that to him. He'd been nothing but good to her. Rescuing her when he wanted to be out there finding his parents' killer. She needed to remember that and not be selfish or disrespectful.

Watching his Adam's apple slide up and down his neck, she backed away just a bit, took his hand in hers and began walking them toward the door. The fresh air would do them both good.

His head glanced down at the ground, and her heart hammered. "You cut your feet."

Her eyes sought where he looked at the smears of blood on the garage floor. She lifted one foot at a time revealing dirty blood smudged bottoms on both feet. She had been so scared she didn't notice till now.

"Yeah," she said stupidly. "I didn't notice, I guess."

He lifted her in his arms, exited the garage and waited for her to pull the service door closed. He turned toward the house, and she could feel the rigidness in his posture. As they walked silently toward the house, he suddenly stopped and motioned with his head to the driveway.

"Do you see those gates at the driveway entrance?"

"Of course."

"The only people that have the combination to get in are Emmy, Dawson, and me. No one else. We change it weekly, so it isn't discovered."

He carried her into the house and set her easily on the kitchen counter, the hard granite cool on her butt. "Stay there, I'll get the first aid kit."

She watched his retreating backside as he walked to his bedroom and disappeared inside. Just a moment later he came out carrying a blue metal box with the red cross on the front of it. No mistaking that.

"Scoot back, so your feet are perched at the edge of the counter, honey." His soft, warm voice wrapped around her and tears threatened her vision at his kindness and gentleness.

He disappeared into the half bath just behind the

kitchen and came out with a gray washcloth which he wetted at the kitchen sink.

"Okay, this might sting a bit, but I have to see how bad the cuts are."

She swallowed, "It's okay, I can just do it my—"

"No. I can do it."

He gently swiped at the bottom of her feet, returning to the sink to rinse the cloth as it became dirty. By the third trip to the sink, he stopped and pulled his phone from his back pocket.

Swiping a couple of times, he pulled up a screen. "This told me someone opened the window in the den. Is that how you got out of the house?" He turned his phone screen to her.

"Yes." Her cheeks flamed a bright pink. "I thought they were in the house."

"It's okay, Megan. I'm just showing you this. I have security all over the place. Every window and door in the house is hooked up to this security system. It's loaded on my laptop, my phone, Emmy's phone, and Dawson's phone."

Just as he said that, his phone rang. He slid the icon to answer it. "Yeah."

Watching the smile spread his lips, her heartbeat revved. Had she ever known there was such a handsome man on this earth? Everything about him called to her, from the breadth of his powerful, wide shoulders to the long leanness of his legs. Powerful thighs encased in his customary denim practically made her swoon when she looked at him. His hair so dark it looked like coal which framed his classic, model perfect face. His dark brows rose into his hairline as he listened to his caller. "Nope, Megan opened the window to get some fresh air."

And he protected her feelings, so no one would think she was a stupid girl.

"Thanks, Daws."

Tapping the icon to end the call, he grinned. "As I said, Emmy and Dawson have the same software on their phones." He checked the bottom of her feet, gently probing the cuts. She winced a bit, and he stopped poking at her sore feet. "When you look around the area alongside the driveway, what do you see?" He pointed to the windows just outside the living room.

Brows furrowed, she looked at the landscape along the drive. "Steep drop offs and rocks."

"Exactly. It's designed that way. It would be hard to climb up here. And, I have sensors all along the driveway and all over my property, so I know as soon as someone turns into the driveway or tries to walk up the drive or the mountain. I have video cameras along the way, and my computer captures every image."

He turned to her, his big hands, rough from working and damp from the cloth, framed her face. "You're safe here. We're safe here."

Licking her dry lips, she had to ask the question. "What about Tamra? Does she have the code? Isn't this still her house too?"

"No. She doesn't have the code and its only her house ... half her house ... in name only. She never wanted to live up here. She hated everything about this place. I think the two years or so we lived up here, she really only spent about five nights total in this house."

"Where would she stay?"

"With her family in town. Or, who knows who she spent her time with."

She couldn't look away from the sadness in his eyes. "Didn't you care?"

He swallowed. "I did at first. But it became clear very soon after we moved in that she was over our marriage and our family."

Family? They had a family. Why that seared her soul, she didn't know. "What does that mean, family?"

He faced her full on, his eyes searching hers and sadness creeped in before a tinge of pride entered. "We have a son, Falcon."

"Oh my God." She whispered as her hand covered her mouth. She shouldn't be surprised, look at him. Most people in their forties had a family, except her. She couldn't bring herself to have children with Waylon. Didn't want them in that environment. Then, as the years passed, she tried to forget about not being a mom. When she'd get down, she'd visit Jolie and hug her littles and pretend she was a mom for just a little while.

His strong fingers tilted her head up. "I'm sorry I didn't say anything sooner."

Swallowing the massive lump in her throat, she inhaled deeply. "It's ... um ... of course, you'd have a family. I just didn't realize."

Setting the freshly rinsed cloth next to her on the counter, he walked to the fireplace and pulled the photo of him when he was younger from the mantle. "This is Falcon, my son."

Falcon. Not Ford. She would never have guessed. They were identical. At least their faces. Handing her the photo, she looked closer and could see Falcon had a scar that separated the eyebrow above his left eye. Glancing up into Ford's face, it wasn't there.

"He's the spitting image of you."

His chuckle said it all. "You have no idea."

"How old is he?"

"He's twenty-five now. Stationed in Afghanistan just outside of Kandahar."

She couldn't look away from the young man staring back at her, the obligatory scowl that all military personnel wore in their pictures. "Thank him for his service, please."

"You can thank him yourself when he comes home." He said it quickly, and her heart tumbled at the idea that she might be here when Falcon returned home. And if she were honest, that sounded really nice. No, great. That sounded great, actually.

His tender smile as he stared at the picture of Falcon crushed her heart. She'd never known what it felt like to grow a child in her womb that had been made from love. Over the years there were times when she broke down from the weight of it. Sitting here now, in the presence of a man she was growing feelings for, it hurt more than ever once again.

His arm muscles bulged and stretched as he set the framed picture in its place on the mantle. Then he turned to her, and her heartbeat sped up once again.

"I believe you wanted to have a talk."

Yeah, she needed to talk to erase these feelings that her heart was breaking.

"Yeah. Um, I just felt I should tell you about Waylon."

He opened the first aid kit and pulled some antibiotic ointment from it and fresh gauze squares.

"Why the change of heart?" His jaw clenched then relaxed, and he kept his eyes on her feet and his task.

"When I was out in the garage, I realized that if I don't tell you everything, you're at a disadvantage to just how serious this all is, and ..."

Squeezing ointment onto his finger, he smeared it over her cuts and her heart hammered at his gentleness. He stayed quiet, and she imagined he was afraid to say anything that might make her stop sharing.

"Waylon stole drugs from Marcus, and that's why he's wanted right now. And by 'wanted,' I think it's not in a good way."

Securing the gauze to the bottom of her feet by wrapping medical tape around the top of each foot and around, he stood and looked into her eyes.

"It's not in a good way if he stole drugs. That could even mean death."

CHAPTER 20

He probably could have eased into the death comment, but he wanted to see her face to see if she still had feelings for Waylon. It irritated the shit out of him that she was even with him in the first place and the more he'd gotten to know her, he realized she was nothing like Waylon. Thank fuck for that.

"Do you mean death as in Waylon or me or both?"

He stood before her, caging her in on the counter with his arms on either side of her and leaned in closer. He could smell her fresh scent again, and his cock came to life thinking about her body pressed against him just moments before. It was time to see just where they were with each other. This playing with a kiss here and there was beginning to drive him mad. If she wasn't interested in taking things further with him, he'd leave here tonight and go find Bobby Ray to put distance between them so his head—and his cock—could get a damn rest.

"I don't know the answer to that. If they think you're lying to them or holding information from them, they could just as easily kill you as him. I don't say that to scare you, but for you to know who you're dealing with. From the intel I have, Marcus works for the El Pablo Cartel. Does that name ring a bell with you? Ever hear Waylon mention it?"

"No." Her lip twisted as she bit at the inside once again.

He could see her heartbeat in her neck, and it was racing right now.

"They're bad news. Mexican. Vicious. And anyone in their way seems to end up missing or dead. You're fortunate they still think you're valuable."

"Oh my God." Her hand flew to cover her full soft lips, her eyes round. "I have to get out of here." She started scooting off the counter, but he held her in place by holding her legs in his hands.

"There's nowhere safer than here, Megan; that's why I brought you here. It's also why I had the cops stop Marcus out of town, so he couldn't follow us."

"But, he can find us. Real estate records are searchable."

"This house and all my land, Emmy's house, and Dawson's house are all owned by LLC's. Our attorney is our registered agent, and our names are nowhere on any documents that trace our companies back to us."

"You all act like you've been through this before," she said softly.

"Honey, my job brings me in contact with bad people. So does Emmy's. For twenty something years, we've had all of our properties protected, and Dawson's just for good measure. We've been careful and deliberate about everything. Sadly, it didn't protect my parents, but they were killed not because of their connection to either Emmy or me but because Dad caught Bobby Ray snooping around their property in the back garage and kicked him out. Bobby Ray didn't take kindly to that and came back that night and torched their house while they were sleeping."

"Oh. My. God." Her hand flew once again to her lips, and the instant tears that sprang to her eyes touched him more than anything else. She felt bad for his parents, and that meant she felt. It was more than he ever got from Tamra.

His heart felt full and heavy at the same time. The thudding of it made him feel more alive than he had in a very long time.

Her delicate, smooth hands then framed his face, her thumbs caressing his cheeks, his eyebrows, the lines he knew were at the corners of his eyes. He swallowed the emotion that lodged in his throat as she continued looking into his eyes. Hers spoke volumes. Need. Emotion. Want. Connection. The green of them the most beautiful color he'd ever seen and which was now his favorite color. He'd paint the den this color if he could match it up, so he could sit down there and feel like she was surrounding him when she was gone.

"Why haven't you divorced?" She said it softly, almost as if she were talking to herself.

Her lips touched his, gentle first, searching, testing. Soon their lips were devouring each other, both of them letting go, tasting, exploring, and enjoying the other. She tasted like freshly brushed teeth—minty and unspoiled. Her recently showered body still held the aroma of the soap in the bathroom and a fresh spring breeze. When her hands dug into his hair and fisted gently, his cock roared to life. His arms pulled her to the edge of the counter, and from this height, the apex of her thighs was right in front of his cock, which strained to break free of its denim prison. Her legs wrapped around his waist and pulled him closer still, and he was lost. He scooped her from the counter, his lips still tasting hers, sliding along the soft wetness of her lips as they molded to his. Had he ever known a kiss could feel like this? Doubtful. This was dizzying.

She moved from his lips and began kissing her way down his jaw, his neck and back up, and he had the presence of mind to tell her what they were about to do to give her a slim chance of saying no.

"I'm taking you to bed, Megan."

"Yes." She hummed it along his neck as she continued to nip and nibble. As they entered his bedroom, he stood alongside his bed and claimed her mouth once more, his hands roaming down to cup her bottom. Her firm globes fit his hands perfectly, and he squeezed, which caused her to bite the tender skin where his neck met his shoulder. The feeling sent blood raging to his cock which grew so impossibly hard he thought it would explode.

Removing one hand from her delicious bottom, he balanced himself with his knee and hand as he moved them to the middle of his bed, pleasure flooding through him when she clung to him with her arms and legs so she didn't fall. Once in the middle, he set her gently down on her back and allowed some of his weight to pin her there while his hands were now free to explore her delicious curves and valleys.

He leaned up just enough to pull his shirt over his head, and her intake of breath was satisfying in itself. She stared at his chest, her fingers roving the hair and warm skin there, enjoying the planes and valleys of his muscles. When her fingers grazed his tightened nipples, she toyed with them, running the pads of her thumbs over each tightened disk then pinching them just hard enough to make his breath huff out.

He reached under her T-shirt and ran his hands over her

warm, soft flesh. He could tell his hands were rough as they skated along her ribs, her stomach, scooting up under her bra and pushing it up to free her breasts. Glancing down, he saw her nipples pucker tighter, and he couldn't resist running his roughened thumb over the tight peaks which caused her to buck.

A slow smile spread across his face; little Miss Megan liked it. Mighty fine, indeed. Pinching the nipple a bit harder, her back arched and her legs wrapped around his as she bucked up into him.

"Oh darlin', we're going to have a good time," he husked out.

His mouth encircled her breast and sucked in hard as the rest of his body enjoyed her bucking and writhing under him. Her legs loosened and tightened around his, and her pussy rubbed against his thickened cock, seeking more.

Moving his head across her chest to her other breast, he continued enjoying her flesh, her movements, her moans. Her hands dug into his hair and pulled him closer to her. He pulled back and lifted her T-shirt over her head; she eagerly helped him, her bra next. Then her hands reached down between them and unbuttoned his jeans. As soon as the button was free, one of her hands dove in and wrapped around his hardness and pumped as much as she could within the confines of his clothing.

"Oh my God. You feel massive. I can't wait to feel you in me."

"Darlin', get your pants off right now."

The smile that split her lips was like a slice of heaven. He lifted only enough to allow her the room to shimmy her pants down. He enjoyed the way her body felt squirming and moving under him, so he wasn't willing to give her more room.

As she pushed her pants down to her feet, she stopped just a moment. "Ford, I don't want to pull the bandages off; help me."

He kissed her lips once more then reared back, moved aside, and pulled her jeans off her feet, leaving the bandages unscathed.

"Oh. Wow." He heard her breathlessly exclaim. Turning to her, her hands immediately roamed over his abs, one of her gentle fingers following the dark hair that trailed from his navel to his cock, which was straining to break free from his jeans. That same soft finger swirled over the head and the glistening pre-cum that had formed at the slit of his throbbing dick, and he thought he'd lose it when she swiped his pre-cum over her lips, then licked it off.

He shoved his jeans over his hips along with his underwear, freeing his cock to slide into her entrance. Reaching to the night stand, he pulled a condom from the drawer and quickly slipped it over, sad that he wouldn't feel her fully.

Swiping his own work roughened finger over her slit, a smile formed on his lips when her wetness gathered on his finger.

"So wet, darlin'. I take that as you're ready."

"Oh, God, yes," she panted.

Hovering over her, his arms on either side of her head, he looked deep into those green eyes and held her gaze as his tip found her entrance. He braced himself there for just a moment, waiting to see if she'd change her mind. She wriggled her hips, so his cock began sliding inside her. Thrusting forward, he entered her, and both of them moaned. Her pussy was hot and wet, and it wrapped around his cock like it was made just for him. Moving slowly, he pulled out and pushed back in, working with her to get a rhythm they both could enjoy. It didn't take more than three strokes before their mating dance began in earnest, her hips rose to meet his thrusts and the movements built that deep tugging and burning in his groin. He continued to stare at her, study her face and her features, and she studied him in return. Each of them committing this to memory as if they were afraid they'd forget it. That would be impossible, though, he was sure of it.

His peripheral vision caught the movement of her breasts each time he planted himself deep within her. Grinding his hips against her clit, she gasped, and he knew he found the right spot. Changing his angle just enough to hit her clit each time he planted himself in her, he watched the color rise on her cheeks. The pink looked fabulous on her. The auburn curls that had loosened from her ponytail splayed out over the bed around her face, and the picture was stunning.

Wanting to hear her moans again, he swished his hips around against her clit and marveled at the way her face changed when she felt the pleasure, her pupils dilated, and her fingers shook against his back. As her orgasm grew, her soft hands reached down to his hips and dug into his flesh, her hips arched higher, and she panted, "Close."

He ground down on her and picked up the pace, he wouldn't release himself in her until she came, but it was going to be close for sure—the tightening in his groin almost painful now. Both of their bodies shined as the sun from the window glinted off their sweaty skin, highlighting the curves and shadowing the valleys.

Her eyes rounded as she looked into his; her smile appeared then disappeared as her lips formed an "o". Her fingers dug into his hips painfully, and she cried out his name, "Ford!"

His name. Fucking fantastic. Five full fast thrusts and he followed her orgasm with his own, his body jerking as his seed spilled from him.

CHAPTER 21

She woke to the chatter and singing of birds, and a heavy arm slung over her waist. The solid chest behind her cocooned her back, the springy hair on his chest both abrading her skin and massaging it. His even breathing, deep and sure, comforted her, and she let her eyes slide closed again. She'd had sex with Ford. Couldn't take it back now, the deed was done. She didn't want to, but what did this mean for their future? Not that there was one. They hadn't spoken about anything past him making her feel safe here in the mountains and then going to find Bobby Ray and Waylon. The thought of that soured her stomach and her mouth. She didn't want him to leave, yet she *did* want Ford to find them and get the justice his parents deserved. No way to do both.

The heaviness that now weighed her chest down caused her breath to hitch. This was just two grown people who were attracted to each other blowing off steam. She'd been through so damn much in the past couple of weeks. She hadn't been touched by a man in more than six years. She'd been waiting for the right man. And she was happy it was

Ford. It felt right that she'd been abstinent, and he'd been the one to break the self-denial.

He'd been through so much for years. Enduring a drug addicted wife, the murder of his parents, and then finding their killer only to lose him again. On top of all that, he had a son fighting in a war on the other side of the world.

The bile souring her stomach increased at the thought of his son. It was stupid for her to feel jealousy, but she did. Trying to analyze it now, she wasn't sure if it was the fact that she didn't have a son or daughter in her life or the fact that Ford had one with another woman. One that didn't want or deserve his love. Life sure sucked sometimes.

Warm, soft lips kissed her tender skin behind her ear. "What's wrong?"

"Nothing."

"Bullshit. Your breathing is irregular, and your skin is clammy."

Well, hell ... in such a short time he'd learned how to read her.

She could feel him raise up on his elbow and his hand cradled her face and turned it back to his. When their eyes locked, his brows rose into his hairline waiting for her to respond. She didn't for long moments, and she saw his jaw tighten, and a hint of scary Ford was beginning to emerge.

"I feel stupid. Jealous. It's wrong and unprovoked, but it's there," she confessed in barely more than a whisper.

"Jealous of who?"

Closing her eyes to block out his handsome face, his hair rumpled by her during their lovemaking ... sex ... whatever.

"Jealous of who?" he asked.

"Tamra, I guess. She was given the honor of your love and of carrying your child."

"Hm. Well, back in the day, I did love her. She was beautiful. Long blonde hair and a face that would stop traffic. Her family was prominent, one of the wealthiest families in Boones County. Her dad runs Amalgent Plastics. And she wanted me. I was enamored with her and couldn't figure it out. Why me?"

She huffed out a breath. "Really? You're handsome, fit, honorable. What's not to like?"

"I didn't run in her circles. They owned the county and everyone in it. When we married, I was still so shocked that I signed every paper put in front of me by her attorney. A prenup, saying I wasn't entitled to any of her trust fund, her father's company, any of the family investments or real estate holdings. Basically, I couldn't touch a single thing they owned. As if I were dirt under their shoes. I couldn't figure it out. Why me then?"

His fingers softly caressed her cheeks, and even though he was looking at her, she got the feeling he wasn't at all.

"It wasn't long into the marriage I realized what a handful she was. Never pleased with anything. Bitchy, unhappy, and demanding. Nothing I did was good enough. I didn't dress right, walk right, talk right. When I continued to work as a bounty hunter, that behavior and her complaints came more often and louder in tone. When she found out she was pregnant, I think a part of her hated that baby growing inside of her. She whined and cried and bitched. It was horrible. She and Emmy almost came to blows many times over the years. Dawson and his wife, Sylvia, can't stand the sight of her.

"After Falcon was born, when I had to go out of town for work, I'd take him to my parents' or Emmy's house. I felt real fear in leaving her alone with him. I didn't think she'd purposely hurt him, but she'd ignore his needs and not take care of him. She started using cocaine when Falcon was one or two. I've never gotten a straight answer, but she hid it well. It took me about five years to really see what was happening. Little telltale signs—she lost weight, her hair became limp and stringy, and the lines around her eyes more prominent. Then I found traces of the powder in the bathroom sink. I've been around it enough to know what it is."

Cupping his face in her right hand, she whispered, "I'm so sorry."

His eyes focused on her again, his gaze intense and dark. "Don't be sorry; it isn't your fault."

Turning, she lifted up on her elbow as she faced him, a sad smile on her face. "I know it isn't, but I've been there. Finding out your spouse isn't the person you thought they were or finding out they never were and you were too self-absorbed to see it."

His fingers tangled in her hair, running through the curls and the look on his face seemed almost marveled at how it felt sliding through his fingers.

"I wanted to resist you, you know. I've sort of found a calm sort of peace in my own little world, and I'm not interested in entanglements. But, the instant I saw you in person, it was like a punch in the gut." His hand moved from her hair to her face, and his thumb roved along her brows, her nose and down her cheek to her jaw. "It's more than your beautiful face—your smile."

He shook his head as if to gather his thoughts and her heartbeat thrummed so fiercely her breath became shallow. She could count on one finger the times a man ever really looked at her like Ford did right now.

"You have a quiet strength that calls to me in some way. Your stoicism is a beacon to my ship. I've read Waylon's file, his rap sheet, and heard you speak about him, and you never feel sorry for yourself. We're the same and different at the same time, you and me."

Her fingers itched to feel the whiskers on his chin, the shadow already growing in the early afternoon. The curly hairs on his chest beaconed for her fingertips to touch them and she didn't resist the call. Lightly touching his chest, smoothing her soft hands over the texture of his skin, a soft sigh left his lips, and she looked up to see his eyes had closed. Gently moving her hand over his nipple, swirling around the dark flat disk, his eyes flew open, and the barely discernible pupils grew large, making those dark orbs darker, almost black. But not sinister—shiny and dark and deep. She saw it now. They held so much emotion in them —tightly leashed and held in check.

"I thought you were scary. At first. You clench your jaw when you're irritated, and that's all I saw at first."

Her fingers gently brushed over his brow and lightly over his eyelids as they closed. "I see now that you aren't always irritated; you're concerned. You care."

When he spoke, it was almost a hiss. "Yes."

"That might be the scariest thing of all."

"Yes."

CHAPTER 22

He slowly rolled her onto her back and cradled his legs between her thighs. It felt right the way their bodies fit together. His firm lines fit so perfect on all of her softness. Her breasts weren't huge, but they were full and heavy and thick. The feel of them as his hands molded and squeezed them sent electric jolts through his body landing on his cock. Tamra had never had that effect on him. She was gorgeous but too thin and boney. He'd been awed that she was interested in him at all, but her body offered no feeling of belonging or rightness. Megan was soft and welcoming and giving.

Touching his lips to hers, he enjoyed the feel of them against his—warm, wet, and inviting. Her lips softened and molded to his perfectly with the perfect amount of pressure and moisture. Her tongue dipped into his mouth and danced with his, both firm and soft and then she swirled it around and gently sucked his tongue between her lips and his cock jumped and thickened painfully. Then she giggled.

"I can feel how hard you are already." Her hips wiggled against him, then she arched up, so her pussy brushed against his hardened cock and the breath flew from his lungs.

"I'm clean. I was tested after Waylon and a couple of times since just to make sure. But I haven't been with anyone else since my divorce."

"Jesus. Megan." He thrust forward, rubbing his rigidness against her soft curls and enjoying the whimpering sounds that came from her chest.

"I'm clean too. I understand if you want me to prove it."

Her shaking head was the only answer he needed. Lifting up just enough to palm his cock, he stroked himself twice, his work roughened hand just enough abrasion that when he slid into her softness, it would feel like heaven. Her legs opened wider in invitation, and her hands cupped her gorgeous tits and lifted them up for him to suck on. Holy fuck.

Eagerly taking a proffered nipple into his mouth, he sucked in deeply and reveled in the sounds she made—part moan, part whimper—from deep in her chest. It almost sounded like she was growling or purring like a cat when it's content.

Kissing across her chest, he sucked the other breast deep into his mouth, and there it was, the purring sound. Her hips arched up, and his hand stilled at the base of his cock until she lowered herself down. Positioning the thick crown of his cock oozing with precum, swirling it onto the seam of her pussy, she reared up again, and he pushed himself inside.

Her hands gripped his waist as he pulled almost all the way out, leaving the firm flared crest seated in her tight grip. Thrusting in once more, her wet heat encased him tightly, and he groaned loudly—the feeling overcoming him.

"Yes," she whispered, and her legs lifted and wrapped around his ass, her heels pressing him to go deeper.

"Jesus," he huffed. Pulling out slowly and thrusting back in just hard enough to make her fabulous tits move, he shifted between watching her breasts and watching her face. Green clashed with dark, and they held as he began pounding into her, their dance becoming fevered and energetic. Her legs tightened and relaxed over and over as she helped him push into her, her hips rising to meet each thrust. As hard as it seemed he'd come faster this time, just for the sake of the familiarity and her eagerness to bring him to spill into her. Just that thought alone made him harder. He could feel his semen spilling into her tight channel, and he pumped harder and faster, her noises growing with each thrust.

She did it again, called his name when her orgasm rolled over her, and he returned the favor. As his seed spilled inside, he whispered, "Megan."

As spots danced before his eyes and his heart hammered in his chest the only thought he had was, what now? Once he found Bobby Ray and Waylon, she'd be safe to go home. He couldn't leave this house, wouldn't. He'd left before thinking Tamra would realize he didn't care that much about it and sign the fucking divorce papers, but a piece of him was here. He was whole here. His stomach knotted. Soft, warm hands smoothed the skin on his back, caressing him, soothing him. With his head tucked into the crook of her neck, he kept his eyes closed for just a moment. Beeping sounded from his phone, and he groaned.

"I hate to say this, but Emmy's back."

Her hands stilled. "How do you know?"

"My phone just told me someone opened the gate. Dawson is working, so it has to be Emmy."

"Shit. Ford, you have to get off me, so I can run to my bathroom. Shit."

Despite the situation, he chuckled and begrudgingly rolled off. She quickly scooted to the edge of the bed and stood, a slight whoosh of air rushing from her lungs as her sore feet hit the floor. She bent to pick up her discarded clothing, and he leaned up to enjoy the view of her backside as she bent and scooped, her perfect flesh wiggling as she ran out of his bedroom door.

Heaving out a deep sigh he rolled out of bed, smoothed the covers on top, then donned his shirt and jeans once again. He walked from his bedroom just as Emmy entered from the garage door.

"Good afternoon."

"Hey. Guess what I found out?"

"I have no clue. You want coffee?"

She lifted her green cup and cocked her head to the side.

"Hi, Emmy." Megan strode from the bathroom, her hair retied on top of her head, loose curls bobbing about as she walked. Her skin was flushed, but her jeans clad legs looked sexy as hell as she walked on the balls of her feet toward the counter, her white bandages peeking from under her jeans. Her gaze fell on him and held as she sat across from him on a stool next to Emmy.

"You want something to drink, Meg?"

"Still some coffee left?"

He nodded and pulled a cup from the cupboard and poured steaming coffee into it. Reaching into the refrigerator, he pulled the creamer container out, poured a bit into her cup then slid it across the counter to her. She smiled at him, and his gut flipped. He winked at her then and hoped like hell he wasn't being a silly school boy and that he affected her close to as much as she affected him.

"Well, it seems you two are getting along just fine," Emmy quipped, and the redness that tinted Megan's cheeks was gorgeous.

"Yeah, we're getting along. Now tell us what you found out." He smiled at Megan again, and the smile she returned was breathtaking.

"Wow, you two. Holy moly." She pulled a file from the shoulder bag she'd hung on the back of the stool she sat on and slid it across the counter to Ford. "Is that Marcus?" She pointed to one of two men standing on a sidewalk carrying on a conversation. It looked like a surveillance photo. Grainy but easy to make out Marcus.

"Looks like him to me." Looking toward Megan, he asked, "What do you think?"

She leaned up to get a better look, then changed her mind and walked around the counter to stand next to him. Bowing her head down to study the picture, he couldn't help studying her. Her neck was slender and creamy, little curls at her nape begged for his fingers. Her shoulders were straight and proud, her posture proper without drooping shoulders. The blue T-shirt she wore tucked into her jeans, and he could see the perfect shape of her ass. Her bare feet added a touch of country girl and a whole lot of sexy.

"That's definitely him. I don't know who the other man is though."

"Ford does." His attention snapped back to his sister, the smirk on her face evident that she caught him thinking carnal thoughts.

"I do?" Looking over Megan's shoulder at the picture, he leaned in just a bit, so he was brushing against her. He smiled when he saw goose bumps form on her arm. He affected her, all right.

"I don't think I do, Emmy."

"Well, maybe this picture will help you." She slid another one across the counter to them, and he peered down at the same man with his arm around Tamra. They were walking into a store and again the photo was grainy but easy enough to recognize the faces.

"Is that Stephano?" He looked a bit closer, then shrugged his shoulders. Stephano had dark hair and dark eyes like him, but he had the olive skin of a man with Hispanic blood.

"Yep."

"Who's Stephano?" His jaw tightened just an instant before forcibly relaxing. "Tamra's boyfriend slash supplier. That's Tamra with him."

He froze as she studied the picture of his ex-wife. Her sweet features long gone and replaced by the lines and sallow skin of a drug user. Her once full thick hair now hung in stringy clumps down her back, her collar bone protruding from her body as if she'd been starved for weeks and was dying. She probably was. She was killing herself every day, and she didn't care. She stopped caring about anything or anyone when she got hooked. Her every waking breath now only brought thoughts of her next hit and partying.

Megan's head twisted to look at him. "I thought you said she was beautiful."

Huffing out a breath, he responded, "She used to be. That's what the drugs have done to her." He pulled his phone out and pulled up a social media site, scrolling through pictures from Falcon's page. He found a picture of Tamra and Falcon taken the last Christmas she was still somewhat sober. Turning his phone to face her, he watched her eyes grow round and large in her head as she realized just what the drugs had done to this woman.

"Oh my God. That's awful." She looked at the current picture again and shook her head slowly as if she felt pity.

"So right," Emmy began again. "So, I found out that Stephano is Marcus' boss."

"What?" They said it at the same time, both looking at Emmy for a response.

"Yep." She splayed more pictures onto the counter, and then a final picture of a man with Marcus that looked like the pictures he had of Waylon.

"That's Waylon!" Megan exclaimed. "So, he was working for Marcus?"

"This picture was taken earlier this year, in January. The DEA has been following Marcus around. They know he's involved with the El Pablo Cartel. He's simply managed to keep himself very clean, but they're watching and waiting for him to slip up. Right after this picture was taken, it seems Waylon decided to help himself to some of the coke they're pushing. Taking small little baggies here and there. But cartels don't screw around. Everything is weighed and weighed again for just this reason. At first, it was only off a gram or so, then it grew to be more. Finally, Waylon got very greedy and took two full bricks. A brick is also called a kilo, and a kilo of cocaine in New York can bring thirty grand or more. I don't have exact numbers from my source as to how much he stole before he got very greedy, but suffice it to say, if they had a buyer lined up beforehand, they could have sold it quickly and be out of the country now. He may have needed it to buy off the guards or other personnel to tell him when the van would be coming through and how to pull off his rescue of Bobby Ray."

Walking to his desk, he pulled up his laptop and began typing away. He had a few databases he could search for airports, boat rentals etc., to find if they left the country or were hiding out. His blood thrummed through his body, excitement edging out his sated feeling after making love to Megan. This was the feeling he loved, searching for his prey, and feeling like he had a lead now just brought that fire alive. He tapped and waited as sites loaded. He pulled his phone from his pocket and dialed Rory's number.

"Yeah."

"Any idea if Bobby Ray or Waylon left the country?"

"They didn't. We had surveillance in every airport, dock, car rental place in the country the second we got word that Bobby Ray escaped."

"Okay. I'm doing some checking myself. I'm home now, so let me know when you hear anything."

He began scrolling the page he'd pulled up on his screen. It was a site run by a former Navy SEAL friend of his, Jared Timm, who was also a conspiracy theorist and had so much intelligence on so many obscure things it was mind boggling. The government really should hire this guy; he knew some serious shit. Only a few select people had the password to access the site, and it had served him well on many occasions. He paid him back by donating to his "cause." A man's gotta eat, after all.

As he read the screen, looking for the section he wanted, he could faintly hear Megan and Emmy chatting away about the soccer game, the weather, clothes, flowers—it didn't matter. What mattered was he had a beautiful woman in his house that he enjoyed spending time with. Her body welcomed his in a way he'd never known before, and his family liked her too. He'd never had that before. And then he sees it, the faint hope that he just might be on to something.

CHAPTER 23

Emmy left, and Ford continued to work at his computer, printing pages here and there, typing notes, and drawing out maps. She watched him for a while, and he seemed to be in a zone, oblivious to her presence. Her stomach growled, and she looked at the clock, surprised to see that it was now two in the afternoon and she hadn't eaten yet. The morning had flown by in a whirlwind, and so did the afternoon. Making them each a ham sandwich, she brought him a sandwich and a fresh cup of coffee to his desk and turned to leave him be when he grabbed her arm and pulled her down onto his lap.

His lips sought hers as his warm solid arms encased her close to him and her arms automatically wrapped around his shoulders as she sunk deeper into his kiss.

He pulled away and touched his forehead to hers. "Thank you."

She kissed his nose, giggled, and replied, "You're welcome."

She stood gently on her sore feet and went to the

kitchen to clean up the small mess she'd made. She set a new pot of coffee on to brew since Ford would likely drink it down by the gallon. Then she searched around the kitchen to make supper plans.

She decided on a homemade bar-b-cue chicken pizza, fresh garlic knots, and a salad. Then she spotted the bag of apples Emmy had brought up and decided to make an apple pie. Nila had taught her how to make the famous pies she made at the restaurant, and the thought of her kind employer made her heart ache just a bit. Jolie promised to go and fill Nila in on what had happened and that Megan would be gone for a while, but she knew Nila depended on her and she felt bad for ditching her like she had. Setting about making her crust, she enjoyed looking across the open concept room and seeing Ford, concentration furrowing his brow, but peace and contentment in his posture as he searched and made headway of figuring out where his prey was hiding. It was exciting watching him.

Cooking for him soothed her, and she felt like she was able to repay him for his hospitality by making him homemade meals and allowing him to work. Her mind kept wandering to what it would be like if this was her life. She'd be content living like this. Working in her beautiful home, her husband thriving and happy. If she still thought it wasn't too late, she'd try and get pregnant. Her heart hammered at the thought that there still might be a chance for her to be a mom. Her hands stilled on the apple she peeled as she remembered that she isn't on birth control, and they hadn't used protection the second time they had sex. Of course, it was highly unlikely that one time and she'd get pregnant, but if they found themselves in the throes of passion again, she should probably be smart about it and ask him to use protection. It wasn't a question of being clean; it was the responsible thing to do to not bring an unwanted child into the world, even though she'd always want a child of her own that had grown in her tummy. She'd longed for it for so many years. Heavily sighing, she finished peeling the last of her apples.

After cutting them up, she coated them with her spices, adding just an extra dash or two of the cinnamon like Nila taught her. Hopefully, Ford wouldn't mind. Pouring them into her crust, she dotted the top with butter, added her top crust, sealed the edges with a perfect zigzag and popped it into the oven. Loading her dirty dishes in the dishwasher, she grabbed the coffeepot and limped over to the desk where Ford continued to work. She filled his cup, her heart hammering in her chest when he looked up at her and smiled. Oh, his smile was sigh worthy. Straight white teeth gleamed, his full soft lips formed the perfect shape, and his features looked soft and serene.

"Are you okay, hon? I'm sorry I'm ignoring you, but I'm making some headway here. Just a bit longer, okay?"

"Oh, Ford, please don't worry about me, I'm fine. But my feet are a bit tender, so I'm going to relax on the sofa a bit, if you don't mind."

His eyes grew large as if he'd forgotten about her feet, then he stood, took the coffeepot from her hand and set it on the edge of the desk, and then scooped her up in his arms. "I don't mind at all; and, in fact, I insist."

He carried her to the sofa, tucked a blanket around her legs, then kissed her softly on the lips. He turned and started a fire in the fireplace, which was a sight she'd love to see every day. His broad shoulders and the muscles in his back straining and pulling as he reached for the wood, stacked it just right in the fireplace and set the flames ablaze with a simple click of the long lighter he used. He put the coffeepot back on its warming plate and sat back at his desk, with a wink in her direction—enough to make a girl swoon.

She watched the fire dance and flicker in its home, so comforting and mesmerizing. The oven timer began beeping, and she realized she'd nodded off. She sat upright, but Ford stood from the desk. "I'll get it; just relax, hon."

She enjoyed watching his backside as he bent to pull the pie from the oven.

"Damn, that smells delicious," he said as he inhaled the delicious aroma.

He set it on top of the stove, and she cocked her head as she watched him stare at it for some time. When he turned, his eyes were glassy as if he were beginning to cry. He brusquely walked to his bedroom and returned a few moments later—composed—as if nothing had happened.

She watched him for a moment, tucking that memory away for another day. Then she noticed a book on the coffee table, a bookmark peeking from the top, which made her smile. She hated when people bent the corners of a book over. The book was a legal thriller, and it seemed he was half way into it by the position of the bookmark. She picked it up and ran her hands over the smooth cover he'd had his hands on too. She should have guessed from the den downstairs that he was a reader. For some reason, this made her immensely happy. She loved reading, though she read a variety of things, romance novels were her go to genre, but legal thrillers, paranormal romance, historical, she loved them all; but a man who reads, now that's sexy.

Her feet raised and then lowered onto his firm thighs as he pulled the blanket back a bit and examined her bandages. He frowned slightly then gently massaged the tops of her feet, at least the parts that weren't covered in medical tape.

His eyes met hers, and he huffed out a deep breath. "I'm going to leave in the morning, I have some good leads on them, and I think I can make this quick. Just one quick question. What was Waylon's mother's name?"

Her heart just broke in two. She knew he'd be going, but it was too soon. They were just beginning to get to know each other.

"Let me go with you." She hated sounding needy. Hated that she just said those words to him.

His perfect lips turned down slightly. "It's not safe, and I don't want you used as a pawn in any way."

"I won't be used that way. I may even be able to help you find Waylon. I can try and touch base with him and flush him out."

"No." His jaw clenched, and she saw his back grow rigid.

Stupid tears flooded her eyes. She cast her eyes down, looking at anything but his handsome face. It was just too good to be true.

"Hey. I'll be back in a few days. Maybe three tops."

His hand tightened on her leg still stretched across his lap. She tried pulling her legs back only to be held in place, his grip not bruising, but firm. "Look at me."

She couldn't. She didn't even know why this was hitting her so hard; it was like the daydreaming she'd had today felt so real and now it wasn't. None of it.

She felt herself being pulled into his lap, his strong firm hands, cupping her face. "What's going on here, Meg?"

Swallowing the knot in her throat—and her embarrassment—she shrugged her shoulders. Afraid she wouldn't be able to say the words correctly. It felt stupid to think she'd fallen or began to fall for him so quickly, but in truth, he was everything she'd ever dreamed of. When he found Bobby Ray and Waylon, she'd be free to go back home, to her burned out, empty house and continue on with her lonely life and that made her so sad. She'd never actually felt lonely before, but she knew she would now. Her dreams of black-haired, black-eyed babies now floating away.

"Hey." He tilted her face up, so she had to look into his eyes—see him. The tenderness she saw there made the tears flow down her cheeks.

"It's stupid, really. I'm just feeling sorry for myself."

He tucked her head under his chin and pulled her tight to his body, the smell of wood and leather seeped into her, and she vowed to remember that smell for the rest of her life.

"Hey there, you knew I was going to be leaving for a while to do my job, right?"

She nodded her head against his chest, and he held her there, his strong arms wrapped around her as if he'd never let her go, but of course, he would.

After a long while, he pulled back to look at her and asked, "Why are you having a pity party?"

Breathing in and letting her breath out, she whispered, "I've never had a man not leave me. I'd allowed myself to believe maybe it would be different with you."

His mouth claimed hers in a hungry kiss. He turned her so she straddled him, his hands now free to roam over her entire body. He kissed her as if he were marking her, leaving an imprint, an impression that would never leave. She kissed him back with the same fervor; she tasted every inch of his hot mouth. Her hands roamed his hair, shoulders, his chest, his abs. She felt the thickness of his cock as it grew against her pussy, and she instinctively rocked against it, eliciting a gasp from him and a thrust of his hips up into her.

Pulling his T-shirt up and over his head, he caught her wrists in his hands, slowly pulled them behind her back and held them tightly with one hand while catching her chin in the other.

"I'm not leaving you forever—just for a few days. Just to do my job."

"Then what?"

"What do you want, Meg?" Oh, how wonderful that sounded. He wanted to know what she wanted. His deep sultry voice, raspy and sexy as it rolled over her skin. Gooseflesh formed, and her nipples furled into tight points. His eyes held hers for a long time, then he let them roam over her body and the heat that filled his features caressed her skin as if he were actually touching her. He let go of her chin and dropped his hand to her nipple, pinching it between his thumb and forefinger, and she moaned. "What do you want, Meg?"

She pushed her body into his hand, but she was held in place by his firm grip on her wrists behind her back. "I'm not above coaxing it out of you." In one swift move, he'd moved her wrists above her head, re-clasped them in his big, strong hand and pulled her T-shirt over her head— releasing her arms long enough to completely remove her shirt. His head dipped in to nip at her neck, the soft spot behind her ear and nip a trail down her shoulder, then back up to her ear. He whispered softly, "Do you want this?"

"Yes," she whispered in response.

He brought her arms behind her again, holding them in one of his hands. His free hand reached around and unclasped her bra, releasing the pressure on her nipples. The same hand then pulled the straps from her shoulders as far as they would fall with her hands still clasped behind her. "Oh, look how hard your nipples are. I think you definitely want this."

A soft tug on her hands behind her back pulled her body back, and her breasts jutted up closer to his face. His tongue softly circled a breast then blew on it, watching it tighten further. A beautiful smile formed on his lips as he watched his handiwork. Then he repeated it on the other breast, enjoying the show. Lavishing gentle teasing attention on her breasts had her squirming in his lap. She wanted it harder, firmer, commanding. She wanted to feel his ardor, his passion. She needed to know he was growing feelings for her as she was for him.

"You have the sexiest breasts. Full and heavy and sexy." He squeezed one with his free hand, testing its weight, the firmness, the texture. "Just perfect."

The backs of his fingers floated down her stomach, gently stopping just above her curls. "And this, your firm yet soft belly. When you press it against me I can feel the fullness of your breasts and the flatness of your stomach and woman, it is so damned sexy."

She whimpered as her body was on fire with his touches and his praise. "And, then there's this paradise right here." He dipped his fingers into the top of her jeans, found them a barrier to touching her wetness, so he pulled his fingers out, unbuttoned the fly of her jeans and tugged the zipper down with one hand. Eagerly dipping his fingers into her wetness, he hit her clit on the way down, and she rocked forward. "This is simply paradise, Meg. Soft and hot and so fucking tight. Did you feel how tight a fit it was when I slid into you? Could you feel every inch of me as I pushed my way inside you?"

"Yes. God, yes."

Her breathing grew ragged, and she could feel her skin flush with want and need. His teasing was a combination of foreplay and frustration. She just wanted him inside of her. Now. He seemed to want to take his time.

"So, I'm going to let go of your hands, and I want you to stand in front of me and shimmy your jeans and panties off. Then, I want you to climb back on my lap. Okay?"

Swallowing, she nodded, because shit, that was hot. He basically wanted her to strip for him and the way she felt right now, she'd do just about anything he asked of her if it meant he'd be in her soon. "Good girl."

He released her hands, placed his on her hips and helped her to her feet. Sitting back to enjoy the show, she thought a little teasing, in turn, would be good for him. Slowly letting her bra fall down her arms, she gathered a breast in each hand and squeezed them, tweaking her nipples, and then gathering them in her hands once again. His mouth dropped open, his eyes glazed, and when she allowed herself to look at his tented pants, the firm outline of his cock was pressed against the leg of his jeans. She licked her lips, and he groaned.

Tucking her thumbs into the waistband of the denim that now felt far too constricting, she wiggled her hips as she slowly revealed her lower body to him. They had sex twice earlier today, but he hadn't had the chance to really look at her. He was enjoying the view now if his rapid pulse pounding in his neck was an indicator. His breathing grew raspy, and if it was at all possible, the outline of his magnificent cock grew more pronounced.

Kicking her jeans to the side, she held her hands out to her side and slowly turned in a circle for him to get a full view. When she was once again facing him, he'd begun shucking his clothing in hyper speed, he shimmied his jeans down his thighs and oh, what a sight that was. He was still fit, defined muscles on his stomach, his corded shoulders and his strong thighs showed her all muscle and not an ounce of fat anywhere on him. Delicious.

His movement was so fast she didn't see it coming, but he placed his hands on her hips and pulled her toward him so quickly she almost lost her balance. Not to worry, he had full control of her once again, and the thought sent a shiver of deliciousness down her body to her pussy.

As she sat straddling his lap, his long thick cock jutted up between them, the slit at the top leaking pre-cum. She began to reach for it, but he pulled her hands behind her once again and clamped his mouth over one of her breasts and sucked in hard. She whimpered and then flushed when she felt the wetness gather between her thighs. As if he knew what she was thinking, he leaned back as far as he could while still holding her hands, and slipped his finger up her slit, smiling as he held his glistening finger up for her to see. As his eyes captured hers, he grinned before licking her juices from his finger, and she thought she'd pass out from the feelings that stirred in her. She wriggled her hips to get closer to his cock, which continued to bob between them, eager to fill her.

"All right, hon, rise up on your knees so I can position my cock to slide inside of you."

This was too much. She'd never been so commanded, so enthralled, and so utterly wet and excited. She could feel the sweat forming at her hairline and between her breasts. The flush of her skin was most certainly a tell of how anxious she was to feel him in her. Then she felt the firm satiny crown of his cock tease her entrance, back and forth, wiping their juices together at her entrance. "Okay, sweetheart—when you're ready, slide down on me. Make it last."

"I don't want it to last. I want to go fast."

"Uh-uh, not this time, hon. I want to remember this while I'm out there on the road. I want to know you're remembering it too." His fingers dug into the side of her hip as she slowly slid down his solid cock. She needed to rise up and lower herself a couple of times before he fit his full length inside of her, but oh Lordy, once he was in her, the fullness she felt was delicious.

"I'll never forget this," she whispered. He let go of her hands, placing his other hand on her hip, working her up and down slower, much slower than she wanted to go, but she had to admit it felt so right.

Watching each other, every nuance of his face, those obsidian eyes, which in the firelight and waning light of the day looked darker than ever, his pupils dilated to the point she didn't know where they ended. His nostrils flared slightly when she impaled herself on his cock, then rocked back and forth to rub her clit against him. One of his hands flew to her clit then, his thumb rolling small circles around her swollen nub. She moaned her pleasure, and he continued working her clit as she continued riding him. He leaned into the back of the sofa and the change in angles hit her front walls, and she could feel her orgasm rushing forward. Her breasts swayed and bounced as she rode his cock, then he put more pressure on her clit, and she exploded. She called his name and moaned into her orgasm, and she heard him whisper, his voice raspy and jerky, "I fucking love that you say my name when you come."

Her legs felt like jelly, but he needed his release, so she braced her hands on his shoulders and moved faster, galloping toward his release. She watched in amazement as his face changed, the adoration she saw in his eyes grabbed her heart as she pumped his cock for all it was worth. His hands gripped her hips so hard, she'd probably have bruises, but it would be worth it. Then he stiffened and groaned long and loud, ending it with her name. He was right about that too; she fucking loved it when he said her name when he came.

CHAPTER 24

He must be dreaming, a vision so lovely he could cry, a scene so dirty and yet so pure and complete he never wanted it to end. Auburn hair tickled his chest as his mouth was claimed by soft sweet lips. A warm tongue floated into his mouth, teased and tasted him so completely and yet intimately that he'd happily allow it to go on forever. That thought flipped his eyes open so fast, dizziness threatened.

There she was, the girl in his dream, his cock still inside her, her warm, flushed body pressed against his, her generous backside still in his hands. The smile she bestowed upon him had his heart racing furiously as if he had run a marathon.

"We're going to leave a mess if we don't clean up soon." Her lips smiled against his cheek as she brushed soft sweet kisses along it, then his jaw, then down to his neck where she inhaled deeply before laying her head on his shoulder.

His arms snaked around her back and pulled her close while at the same time lifting his hips to keep his softening erection inside her just a minute longer.

His heartbeat thrummed strong and fast in his chest, and it reminded him that for so long he hadn't felt alive, not really alive in that way each day brought a measure of excitement as well as work and play in the daily routines one's life held. He'd been half a man for years, so many years. Why hadn't he realized it until now? He'd never thought of himself as unhappy, but as he thought of it now, he'd not truly been happy either. He existed. Now he had met Megan, and she brought with her so much more than most women. A slightly sordid past, an ex-husband that had little to no morals and definitely lived on the wrong side of the law, and no real family to speak of—they'd all left her. She was everything he wasn't. Except for the miserable ex. But he was close to his family. Would she be able to insert herself into that? Sometimes when you've been alone so long, it was difficult to try and live with people again.

Thoughts trickled through his head. Should he give up on locating Bobby Ray and let the authorities do it? He could turn over his research and let them have it while he explored, really explored what this could mean with Megan. But that wasn't him, and he couldn't let his family down like that. They were depending on him, and in truth, he'd always hate that he didn't go and find that asshole. It would be something that would always grate on his nerves. Plus, he owed it to his parents. While their death had made him a very wealthy man, he wouldn't live on that wealth as he had intended if he didn't do everything in his power to let them rest in peace.

Holding Megan close, he twisted so they lay on the sofa, him on top of her. He kissed her softly then pulled out of her with a groan and quickly stood and walked toward the bathroom to get them a washcloth. "Stay there, hon; I'll be right back."

When he reentered the living room, the sight of all that thick auburn hair splayed across the pillow on the sofa made his heartbeat skip. Taking in the sight of her voluptuous naked body, her skin creamy and smooth, her tummy flat but not so much so that her hips bones protruded, her long shapely legs stretched out, she was simply everything he'd ever wanted, physically. The fact that she cooked, was funny, seemed sweet and caring and a little bit lonely sealed the deal for him. They were so much alike and yet so different.

Changing his mind about the washcloth, he scooped her up in his arms and carried her to his bathroom. He set her on the counter, reached into the shower to warm the water and then knelt to undo the bandages which had spots of blood on them from her standing in the kitchen cooking.

"You must have broken open one of your cuts from standing in the kitchen this afternoon. I think you better take it easy for a day or two to let these begin to heal."

"I'm not used to sitting around; I normally don't have the time for it."

Tossing the used bandages in the wastebasket, he kissed her lightly on the lips. "Now you do."

He lifted her once again, delighted when she gave a little squeal, then stepped into his large shower. For the first time since he'd built this house and insisted on this lavish shower, he was extremely happy he had it. Dreams can come true if you let them.

―――

Megan began making a pizza for them, and he needed to talk to Dawson about it all. He was honestly torn about what to do about her. He felt horrible leaving her here, but that had been the point all along. He didn't count on having feelings at all; he'd simply felt sorry for her. But now he was afraid his feelings had turned into so much more than just liking her, and that made it more difficult. She was in such a vulnerable position right now. She'd lost her house, and she was being targeted and clearly had no one to turn to, so he needed to remember that before he fell deeply in love with her because her feelings could change once life returned to normal. Why did that hurt so much?

"Meg? Honey, I'm going to step out to the garage and pack up my bike for tomorrow. You okay for a bit?"

Pulling her bottom lip between her teeth, he watched as she forced a smile before replying, "Sure."

Nodding, he walked out the back door and through the attached garage. Darkness had set over the mountain now and the lights from the buildings and houses at the bottom of the hill shined like stars from below. He paused for just a moment to admire the view. One of the best things about living up here was his view, both in terms of security and in terms of breathtaking—morning and night.

Continuing on to the garage, he pulled his phone from his back pocket and called his brother.

"Yeah."

He chuckled. "Hey, Daws, you got a minute?"

"Yeah. How's your houseguest?" There was laughter in his voice.

"Been talking to Emmy?"

"Yeah." Chuckling on the other end of the phone made him smile.

"So, then you know. But it's also the reason I'm calling. I feel like I have a bit of a dilemma here. She's vulnerable right now, has no one, and it seems like anyone who's ever been in her life has just up and left. Now it looks like I'm doing the same, and I don't mind telling you it's sitting hard in my gut. I don't want to let her down, but I don't want to let you and Emmy down either."

A full-on belly laugh sounded on the other end of the phone and it both grated his nerves and made him chuckle in return. Dawson always saw the humor in every situation.

"So, you've fallen for her. Emmy said as much, and I must say I'm so fucking happy you're moving on from that crack whore you're married to. Get that bitch out of our family once and for all, Ford."

"I didn't say I'd fallen for her—"

"Right, you didn't, but you have, or this wouldn't be a dilemma."

Sitting in the driver's side of the old Jeep, he gripped the steering wheel with his free hand and closed his eyes as he rested the back of his head against the back of the seat.

"You can't admit it yet?" Dawson chuckled again. "Damn, Ford, you've got it bad, and you're trying to ignore it. Emmy said she's beautiful, sweet, smart, and funny. What the hell is wrong with you? You can't possibly still be carrying a torch for the boney bitch you're married to. Please tell me that isn't the case."

"Of course, I'm not carrying a torch for her. I can't stand the thought of her at this point. And it has absolutely nothing at all to do with her."

"Then who does it have to do with? Falcon wants you to be happy just like the rest of us."

Inhaling deeply, he opened his eyes and imagined his dad standing in front of the Jeep looking at him, a crooked smile on his face telling him he was being a fool in so many ways right now. "I guess it's happened so fast that it seems wrong or weird or something."

"Please remember that I asked Sylvia to marry me on our third date. Dad asked Mom to marry him on their second date. Sometimes it happens fast. There's no perfect time frame in which a person is supposed to fall in love. And you'll hate yourself if you don't go and bring Bobby "Fucking" Ray in to be tried for killing Mom and Dad. And, if she can't stand that you go and bolts or wants to not see the truth of the matter, she isn't the right one for you. So, now what?"

"Right." He hefted himself from the Jeep and began walking toward the other side of the garage and his bike. The decision was clear; he had to go. "I'll leave in the morning to go find Bobby Ray, and then when I come home, I'll see how Megan feels about me. In the meantime, will you and Emmy watch out for her while I'm gone? She'll be all alone up here."

"Brother, we'll all stop in daily and make sure she's doing fine. Maybe she'll want to babysit, and Sylvia and I can actually get a date night in."

"Shit, Daws, you've already got her watching your kids?"

Laughter sounded on the other end of the phone before he said, "Gotta go, bro. Be careful out there and come home safe."

Ending the call and tucking his phone into his pocket, he uncovered his bike, a 2014 Dyna Low-rider. He still remembered the day he'd picked it up from the dealership, the first brand new bike he'd ever bought, and it felt like freedom. Taking a trip down Main Street in Lynyrd Station, people stopping and waving, the smile on his face grew from ear to ear. Then, he drove past the cottage he'd been staying in, turned onto his mountain road, and felt exhilarated that this house was his. He vowed he'd get it out of Tamra's name, and then he'd gotten the call from Rory—they had a lead on Bobby Ray June, and they needed his help.

CHAPTER 25

Pizza was in the oven, a salad was made, the wine was opened and breathing, so all she needed to complete supper was Ford. And, she'd be a good girl and not complain about him leaving. She knew he had to and that had been the plan all along. He wasn't leaving her; he was going to work. After that, she'd be free to go home, fix her house, go back to work, and she could call Ford and stay in touch with him. If they wanted to get together, it could easily be accomplished on the week-ends or something. Ninety miles wasn't across the country.

The back door opened, and she turned to watch Ford walk into the kitchen, the sight of him always stirring her in the most delicious way. Even now before seeing him her nipples pebbled tightly, her stomach fluttered, and her panties dampened. Such a silly schoolgirl she was. When his dark head poked around the corner, it was even more exciting. Those black eyes reflected the lights from the kitchen, and his full lips parted in a sexy ass smile which made her heartbeat speed up.

"It smells fantastic in here, Meg. How long before supper's ready?"

She glanced at the timer on the oven. "Ten minutes."

"Okay, then let me show you a couple of things you need to know." He sauntered over to his desk, lifted the top on his computer and waited for her to join him. Bonus that he pulled her down onto his lap. Definite bonus.

"Okay, this icon right here?" He used his mouse to point to a red triangular icon with MS in white letters on it. "This is my security system." Double clicking the icon, she tried ignoring the purely masculine aroma wafting from him every time he moved. The software opened to a screen filled with buttons and videos playing from different vantage points around this property.

"These are from all the cameras around the house and on the property. I own this whole side of the mountain. These cameras are placed to allow for viewing from the beginning of the property line at the bottom of the mountain to the end of the property line at the top. For the most part, they sit like this, showing nothing but the scenery, but as soon as something moves in front of a camera, they all turn on and record everything. Even animals trigger the cameras, the smallest squirrel can trigger one of them. What this means is that you will be able to see if someone is approaching the house anywhere on the property."

He pulled a phone from the top drawer of his desk. "This is a private phone and is not traceable to me or you or this house. You can call me or Emmy or Dawson, and if you need me to program anyone else's number into it, I'm happy to do that, so long as you don't tell anyone where you are. This is for your protection, not to keep you a prisoner. Okay?"

"Okay." The butterflies in her stomach took flight. He was keeping her safe.

He tapped Emmy's name on the phone and tapped the speaker icon. "I'm here," she answered.

"Okay, come on up slowly please."

Emmy's SUV triggered a camera, and her vehicle came into view as she drove up the driveway. Then all of the cameras came to life, showing her the entire property. Trees, flowers, mountainside, and the driveway. A beeping sounded from the computer when she was about halfway up the drive. "That tells you someone is approaching."

The beeping sounded faster a few moments later. "That tells you she's approaching the gate."

She watched the video as Emmy stopped at the gate, extended her hand out the window and entered the password on the security panel. The sound of a doorbell then rang from the computer and also from inside the house somewhere. "That's letting you know the gate has been opened."

He held up the telephone he'd just given her. "And if you aren't at the computer, you can see it all right here on the phone." The screen had filled with the images of the cameras she was looking at on the computer screen, one at a time showing her camera after camera, but in the corner was the red button flashing. Ford pointed to that button. "This tells you the gate has been opened."

"Okay. Wow, you weren't kidding you've got this place secured."

"I choose to believe that I'm not paranoid, just safe, but I suppose an argument could be made other than that."

A whistle sounded from the phone and the computer at the same time. "Emmy just opened the garage door." And the screen on the phone flicked to Emmy walking into the garage. She waved up at the camera before entering the door.

"Okay, all good?"

They both turned to see Emmy's smirk as she glanced their way. "Wow, can't you two separate for a moment?"

"Hush, Em, I'm simply showing Megan the security system. And you're a fine one to talk."

His dark eyes caught hers, "Em and Scott can't keep their hands off of each other."

She chuckled. "It smells great in here; what are you making?"

"Bar-b-que chicken pizza, and I made an apple pie earlier."

"Wow, I'm a bit jealous now."

She stood, winced a bit, then limped once as she walked toward Emmy. Ford quickly wrapped his arm around her shoulders and helped her take the weight off her foot. She hadn't been a nurse for a few years, but she'd need to take a look at her feet soon. He hadn't let her look at them before. He pulled one of the barstools away from the counter and motioned for her to sit down. "Meg cut her foot on the stones outside."

"Why the hell were you walking around outside without shoes on?"

"Never mind, Emmy."

Emmy's dark eyebrows rose into the bangs that framed her petite face, her dark eyes the spitting image of her brother's.

"Hm," she grumped, then walked to her brother, wrapped her arms around his waist and pulled him in for a long hug. "Be careful out there. It's more important to come home safe than bring that scumbag back, but I hope you get him."

Ford hugged his sister back, kissed the top of her head and replied, "I'll do both; I promise."

Emmy pulled away, looked directly at her and said, "You call me if you need anything. I'll bring groceries up in a couple of days. Text me what you need, and I'll pick it up."

Patting her brother on the chest a couple of times, she turned and exited as quickly as she entered. That woman was always on the go.

Ford turned to her, his eyes slightly glassy, and her heart raced. "Marge. Margaret June. You asked me earlier, and I didn't get the chance to respond. Waylon's mom's name was Margaret June."

He hurried to his computer and tapped away at the keys as the oven timer sounded. She walked on the outside of her feet to keep from ripping open her cuts, pulled the pizza from the oven and turned it off. Digging around in the drawers, she located a pizza cutter and sliced it in eight pieces. Working as efficiently as she could with minimal walking, she pulled the salads and dressing from the refrigerator and took them to the table. Turning to the counter she managed the salads, and Ford appeared beside her, picking up the pizza with the pot holders sitting alongside and carried it to the table.

"Did Marge have an old hunting cabin in the woods about fifty miles outside of South Pass?"

Oh my God, she'd forgotten about that stupid cabin. "Yes. Shit, I forgot about it. Is that where you think they are?"

"It's where I'm going to start looking. I found it in the real estate records. It was actually an accident. There is a tax deficiency on it. Looks like no one paid taxes on it for about five years now, so the county is foreclosing it out to make themselves whole."

"Oh, wow. Waylon used to just love going hunting every

year, and that's where he went. I can't believe he'd just let that place go. Bobby Ray either."

"Well, whatever is going on with those two, it appears they've changed their minds about that hunting cabin."

Eating in silence for a few moments, she glanced at him often. His thoughts seemed very far away. "I'm sorry I didn't trust you before."

When he looked up at her, butterflies came to life in her tummy again. The light from the fixture above them gleamed in his dark coal black hair. The stubble on his jaw and chin gave him that scary Ford appearance, but she was no longer frightened of him. She now knew better.

"I don't blame you, Meg. In your shoes, I wouldn't have trusted me either."

Nodding, she set her napkin next to her plate. "Ready for pie?"

CHAPTER 26

The apple pie was just as good as his mom used to make. This woman is just too good to be true. Emmy would tell him if it's too good to be true, it probably is, so this would be his secret for a while. Scooping her up from the table where they still sat too full to move, he gently set her on the sofa, jabbed at the fire a bit to get it roaring to life and kissed her on the forehead.

"I'll clean up, then we'll sit and relax."

She started to protest, but he shook his head. Her full lips parted in a blindingly beautiful smile, and his body quickly set itself to blazing. She was impossible to resist.

Heading back to the kitchen, his phone began playing the Wicked Witch theme song. Pulling it from his back pocket, he groaned. Tamra's name and a picture of the witch appeared as her avatar. He tapped "ignore" and silently swore under his breath. She hadn't called him in more than two years now. It figures just as soon as he found someone new, she'd crawl above ground and become a menace.

Making quick work of the dishes, he wrapped up the leftover pizza, covered the pie, refilled their wineglasses and brought them into the living room. As he handed the glass to Megan, he was once again pulled in by her alluring smile framed by her shiny, auburn curls. It never ceased to take his breath away. Their fingers brushed, and he noticed her breathing hitch. Hiding his smile, he gently sat next to her, careful not to jostle her wineglass. As he bent forward to grab the remote for the television from the coffee table, his cell phone rang. Closing his eyes, he silently prayed it wasn't Tamra, but as he glanced at the screen, he again saw the witch staring back.

"I'm sorry about this, Meg." He couldn't look at her, not when he was about to talk to his wife. "What do you want, Tamra?"

He felt Megan begin to scoot away, but he quickly set the hand holding his wineglass on her knee, which thankfully halted her progress. Leaning forward to set his wine on the coffee table, he inhaled deeply, slowly sat back, and circled his arm around Megan's shoulders. It was pure selfishness on his part. He needed the support to get through this phone call which would probably be another of Tamra's rantings about the stupid fucking house on the mountain and why was he so fucking stubborn?

"Stephano told me you're shacking up with one Megan June at MY house. What do you have to say about that?"

"What the hell are you talking about? And where would Stephano get any information about me and who I'm with and why would he give a shit?" He tried keeping his voice even, but it didn't seem to be working. The stiffness in his spine and the dread filling his stomach were the first two warning signs things could get off track in a nanosecond.

"It appears you didn't give your little plaything a proper lecture on safety first, turning her phone off and such things. Marcus was able to track her easy enough."

Slowly, he turned to look at Megan. Her confusion showed on her face, and her brows furrowed slightly as she took in his posture, tight jaw, and immediate fear. He held up a finger to his lips, silently telling Megan to be quiet, tapped the speaker icon on his phone and spoke slowly.

"Excuse me, say again?"

"Oh, for crissakes Ford, I know your little game. You didn't tell your latest plaything to turn her fucking phone off, and now we all know she's up there. So, I want to know what the fuck is going on in MY house, and I want to know now."

He mouthed to Megan, "Where's your phone?"

Immediately her hands flew to cover her mouth, her eyes grew round, and she sat straight up. Slowly she rose to her tender feet and hobbled to her bedroom. He followed her silently, and when they entered the door, he watched as she pulled her cell phone from the top of her purse, already turned on and emitting signals for all the world to track.

He snatched it from her hand and turned it off, though it was a bit late now. His focus back on Tamra, he tried to lie. Smooth as silk he replied, "Tamra, I'm not sure what shit you're on these days or how much of it, but this is MY house, and it always will be. You don't live here, and you never really have. You also will never live here; of that, I will promise. Now, I don't know what or who Megan is, but you need to get off the shit and start thinking straight. Am I clear?"

Laughing sounded on the other end of the line, and he heard Stephano bark at her to hang the fuck up. The line soon went silent, and he turned to Megan, tried like hell to soften his face, but that proved to be impossible.

"What the hell, Megan? I told you to keep your phone turned off. How long has it been on?"

The tears flowed down her cheeks, and her soft full lips trembled. "Since this afternoon. I tried calling Jolie after you stormed out of the house. Then I thought I'd pack and leave since I seem to make you so angry, but I couldn't get a signal. I went downstairs to grab my clothes, and that's when I heard them. You. And got scared and bolted. I'm so sorry. I forgot."

He took in her room. Her bag was on the bed, filled with clothes. Her purse was sitting alongside, and it did indeed look like she'd been planning on leaving, and that thought sat like a hot stone in his belly. She was going to leave.

He turned slowly, left the room, and immediately sat at his computer. Making sure all of the systems were in place and turned on, he picked up his phone and dialed his friend, Rory.

"Yeah."

"I may have a problem." He filled Rory in on the situation and closed his eyes as he listened to his friend tap on his keyboard.

"Yep, Marcus is in town, but that could just be because he has to report in to Stephano. It could also be because he's hoping to see Megan or Waylon or both."

"Right. I've got to give this some thought. I was going to leave tomorrow morning to go back to South Pass and find Bobby Ray. I can't leave her here alone, and I don't want to take her. I'll give you a call later once I've had some time to process this and figure out what I'm going to do."

"Yep. In the meantime, let me see if I can ping her phone. Do you have your scramblers on?"

"Yeah." He raked his hand through his hair once more, trying to keep the bile quickly souring his stomach to settle. He turned Megan's phone back on so Rory could try to ping it.

Megan disappeared into her bathroom, and his eyes scanned his computer screen, looking for any signs things looked amiss.

"Yeah, I got it, Ford. Its signal is weak, but your scramblers aren't completely scrambling her signal. What do you think the odds are that they put something on her phone to make tracking her easier?"

"Fuck, I didn't think of that." His stomach twisted.

"Okay, so log on to Jared's site and type in this IP. 234.342.777.365S. Then put Megan's phone number into the search box. It'll tell you if there's anything in her phone tracking her."

Typing furiously, he added her number and watched the mind numbing little circle turn, fear crawling into his very core. A bright red box appeared on the screen that said in all capital letters BUGGED.

"Fuck. She's been tracked. I should have thought of that. Goddammit."

"Destroy the phone. I don't know what they're using, and we don't have the time to figure it out. Smash the damned thing into pieces and keep Jared's software up. It'll disappear when the phone is no longer traceable."

Jumping up from his chair, he practically ran to the garage and pulled a hammer from his toolbox. He wrapped her phone in a shop rag and began smashing her phone into tiny pieces, letting his anger fly.

Walking back into the living room to check his computer, he watched as the red box disappeared. "The tracking box disappeared. Can you try to ping it again?"

Typing on the other end sounded, and he looked up to see Megan still hadn't come out of the bathroom. She was probably scared and mad as hell at herself. It was a careless mistake but one that his own son had made more than once, which is why the scramblers had come into play. But, in this case, it didn't matter, they were tracking her anyway.

"Nope, no signal now. What are you going to do?"

"I think we'll leave tonight. Heading back to South Pass. The sooner I find that piece of shit Bobby Ray June, the sooner we'll all be safe. By the way, Megan told me Waylon stole drugs from Marcus, so those are floating around somewhere too. My hope is finding Bobby Ray will find Waylon, and the drugs and Megan will be safe. It's a lot of hopes I have right now."

"Right. I'll call Emmy and fill her in; she'll take care of the house. Keep in touch and let me know you're both safe."

"Yeah, thanks, Rory."

CHAPTER 27

Oh. My. God. What in the world had she done? All of his hard work and effort to keep her safe, them safe, and she'd thrown it away feeling sorry for herself. Mortified wouldn't begin to explain how she felt right now. Ignorant. Dumb. Selfish. Were there other words? Plenty.

When he turned and walked out of her room, she wanted to scream and cry. Of course, that would do no good at all. She could hear him on the phone now with Rory, so she stepped into her bathroom. Looking at herself in the mirror, she saw her auburn hair curling in every which way, the humidity making it bigger than it had been in years. Her eyes had bags underneath, her lips too full and puffy. All in all, she hated the woman looking back at her.

Turning the water on in the shower to warm, she decided to take a quick warm shower and get dressed in fresh jeans and T-shirt then she'd offer to leave. She'd tell Ford she could hop on a bus to her brother's in California— surely, she'd be safe out there.

Undressing quickly, she stepped into the warm water, and a shiver skittered down her spine. How did people who loved drama in their lives stand this? She felt like she'd aged ten years in just a week. Washing her hair, then her body, she rinsed, dried herself off and donned her clean clothing. Pulling her hair back in a haphazard braid, some tendrils not minding her ministrations and curling around her face, she inhaled a deep breath and stepped out into the living room to face his wrath. She deserved it.

Stepping into the living room, she saw him sitting at his desk, typing away on his keyboard, engrossed in once again trying to keep them safe. "I'm so, so sorry Ford. Honestly, I didn't even think about it. I'm not used to this. It's not an excuse—not a good one anyway, but please forgive me."

He looked up at her from his computer and let out a long breath. "Come here, Meg."

She took small, tentative steps. He'd shown no violence toward her, but this was just the stuff that would make Waylon snap and throw things. He'd only hit her once, and that was the last year they were married, which was just one more reason to get away from him. As if there needed to be more than she already had.

Once she reached the edge of his desk, she stopped, searching his face for signs of his mood. His brows furrowed as he watched her. "I'll never hurt you. Ever."

She swallowed, placed her hand on her tummy and stepped closer to him, alongside his chair. He reached over and wrapped his hands around her hips and set her down on his lap. Resting his chin on her shoulder, she heard him breathe in her scent, then rest his cheek next to hers. His arms tightened around her waist before he spoke.

"I had to destroy your phone." She sucked in a breath, her head spinning slightly. "Marcus had a tracking device attached to it, and we didn't have the time to figure out how to disable it. So, it wasn't the fact that you left your phone on as much as they've been tracking you all along. It explains how he knew you were at Jolie's and when you were at work and when you weren't. It's also how he knew you were here and just happenstance that his boss is my ex's fuck buddy."

Her lips trembled. "Okay." What do you say to that? She'd never in her life been in a situation like this.

"So, go in your room and pack up all of your things. We're leaving tonight. I've emailed Emmy and Dawson and explained a bit of what's going on. Rory will fill them in on the rest. He found us an Airbnb to stay in tonight, which is in the heart of downtown South Pass, and easily accessible to the police. He also has alerted patrols that we'll be there, and they'll be watching for Marcus' car and any of his colleagues."

Turning in his lap, she looked into those black depths, for comfort and to make sure he wasn't angry. She held his gaze for a long time, and he held hers. His hand cupped her jaw, his thumb swiped over her bottom lip once before he added, "I'll keep you safe. I promise."

"I'm not your responsibility, Ford. I seem to keep pulling you away from your work and completing your mission, and for that, I'm truly sorry."

"You are my responsibility, Megan. It seems I've developed feelings for you, and for that, I'm not sorry." His lips brushed hers gently, and her tummy flipped. "Okay, go pack, and I'll do the same, we've got to hit the road. Rory and a couple patrols will be at the bottom of the mountain in about twenty minutes to make sure we don't have problems leaving town."

Standing, she swiped her hands down her thighs to dry the sweat that had gathered. She walked to the first aid kit still on the edge of the counter and pulled a couple of Band-

Aids from the box, sat on a stool and bandaged up her cuts, then went to the basement to get her clothes long forgotten in the laundry room. As she descended the steps, she turned to see Ford watching her, scary Ford long gone and this new Ford, sweet and protective, watching her movements as if he couldn't look at her enough. The thought of that was so nice it made her heart flutter, and her lips trembled with a soft smile. Things were bad, but they could be so much worse.

CHAPTER 28

Packing was easy for him. He'd done it so many times in his life and for extended periods. Often, he'd leave home and not know how long he'd be gone. This was just another one of those times, but it was the first time he was bringing someone along with him, and this someone had become special, so that explained his sudden nerves. Grabbing his duffel bag, he headed to the desk and gathered his notebook and the maps he'd been compiling. Megan exited her bedroom, and he motioned with his head to the garage. She'd put on shoes, and he noticed that she was walking on the outside of her feet. Another dilemma was she wouldn't be able to run if they needed to. He'd have to keep that in mind as they made their way toward Bobby Ray.

Double-checking the security systems on his laptop, he closed the lid and laid it in the drawer, locking it up. The lights were on timers and would go off at different times each night, and if they were watching, Marcus and Stephano wouldn't know if they were inside or not. Closing the blinds on the windows, he quickly made his way to the garage and tossed his bags into the back seat of his truck.

Megan had already settled herself in the passenger seat, her head turned to watch him from over the seat. He caught her gaze. "I'll be right back, please stay here."

She nodded but didn't vocalize her acceptance, and he hoped that was due to fear and not that she had no intention of complying with him. He swiftly made his way to the back garage, pulled his weapons from the bags and hiding places on his Harley, strapping them to his waist, ankle, breast holster and one for the console holder in his truck. Locking up the doors, he scurried to the garage and let out a breath when Megan was still sitting still as a mouse in the passenger seat.

As Ford backed out of the garage, she watched as the door came to a close before them, then turned his truck and headed down the side of the mountain. His eyes scanned the area for signs of anyone approaching, any danger, or movement, and his back was stiff and tight. Navigating a sharp corner, he pulled his phone from his back pocket and with a quick flick of his wrist, set it up in the holder on his dash. Tapping the MS icon, he flicked his gaze between the road and his phone, making sure the security system was working. Maneuvering around another corner, his headlights scanning the area for him, his relief at being close to the bottom and not seeing signs of anything out of the ordinary helped his breathing regulate. Megan sat perfectly still, probably nervous on the mountain road at night and the whole situation, but for right now, he was grateful for her silence.

His phone rang, and he tapped the Bluetooth connection on his steering wheel. "Montgomery."

"Rory here. Marcus is still at Stephano's, and so far, we haven't detected any minions running about. I'm down here waiting."

"We're almost there. Five minutes."

The call ended without any further conversation. It was how he and Rory communicated, no extra bullshit needed.

Rounding the final corner, he saw his friend's headlights at the end of the drive and felt immensely better for it, but they were far from safe at this point. Who knew what Stephano had planned? This in itself was most likely a trap.

Megan let out a long-held breath and voiced his concerns. "This might be a trap to get us to move."

"It might."

"Do you—do we have a plan B?"

"Nope."

"What's your plan with all the security at the house and all over your land? What would you do if someone breached it?"

"I'd get ready to kill them. At the very least defend myself and anyone in the house. But, I couldn't leave you there alone without my protection, and my hope is that they won't expect me to move so quickly. I think we have the time advantage."

Her slight nod was the only acknowledgment of his comments, so he took it. As he neared his best friend, he flashed his brights once, which glistened off the sleek black Charger his friend just loved above all other cars. When he'd made detective, it was the first thing he bought. The department paid for his gas and insurance, but he bought the car, so it was his and he didn't have to share it with anyone else.

Rory backed up to let them pass, and he turned onto the road that would lead them out of Lynyrd Station. A few things he knew for sure at this moment in time were that he'd come back to this house for good once this was over and he was finished with bounty hunting. It was time he lived life instead of existing in it. What he wasn't sure about was if Megan would be in his life. That thought made his gut twist.

"How would Marcus get a tracker on my phone?" Her soft voice pierced his thoughts.

"I don't know. I wanted to talk about that. Would there have been any time when you thought someone had been in your house? When something was out of place? A feeling?"

His heart raced as he waited for her answer. When he glanced briefly at her, he saw the moisture in her eyes reflected from the ambient light from his phone.

"There was a night that I thought Marcus was on my front porch. I thought I heard something and looked out the window and saw his car out front. My heart was beating so fast I could barely breathe. But I didn't think he'd come in the house. I got up and locked my bedroom door and listened for movement in the house, but I didn't think I heard anything."

"Had you been sleeping?"

"Yes." Her one word was so soft he could barely hear it.

"Could he have been in your house before you woke and you heard him leaving?"

The glint of a tear sliding down her cheek and falling on her lap caused an instant tightness in his throat. Her shoulders lifted and fell silently. "I don't know."

"Did you sleep with your phone by the bed?"

Shaking her head no, her breath caught in her throat. "I usually left it in the living room on the charger by the sofa."

He reached across the console of his truck and took her hand in his. Squeezing it tightly, he held on trying to give them both comfort. Marcus had gone so far as to gain entry into her home while she slept. Putting a tracker on her phone was the least of the things he could have done to her —something she was already realizing.

CHAPTER 29

Weak and nauseous. There was no other way to describe how she felt right now. The level to which she was in over her head muted her. And, to top it off, she'd done nothing wrong other than having been married to that asshole, Waylon. If she had a crystal ball right now, she'd wish herself back to the day she'd met Waylon and change it all. Everything.

They trudged up the steps to the apartment on the third floor of an older building in South Pass. The business below was a tiny card shop run by a nice hippy type lady named Sunflower. She'd met her years ago when her grandmother was still alive, and they came shopping for cards. Sunflower's cards were handmade, unusual, and pleasing to the eye. Some of her sayings inside were obscure and weird, but the cards with the blank insides were the ones she usually purchased. Sunflower lived on the second floor, and she'd turned her third-floor apartment into an Airbnb for extra income. Not a bad gig for a hippy.

Ford unlocked the door, and the welcoming feeling that washed over her actually soothed her nerves. Earth-toned furnishings and all colors accented the brightly colored paintings of sunflowers, of course, and other florals that she'd guess were actually painted by Sunflower herself. Not something she'd ever have in her own house, but for some reason, this worked beautifully. She stepped farther into the living room, and Ford stepped in behind her, set his bags next to the sofa and looked out the window before closing the blinds. The apartment was small with an open concept. The small, but quaint living room floated into the kitchen area which was no more than a small bank of cabinets with colorful orange and yellow flowers inlaid within blue tiles. The cabinets were painted gray and complimented the living room perfectly. A short hallway led to the bathroom and then the bedroom toward the back. Setting her bag on the queen-sized bed she took in the decorating of the bedroom, much the same as the rest of the apartment. Sparsely furnished but comforting. Ford followed her into the bedroom, went straight to the window overlooking the back alley behind the building and closed the blinds.

He pulled his phone from his back pocket and tapped an icon. "We're here. It looks safe enough, and I'll install the portable motion sensors on the first and second flights of stairs. Thanks for your help, Rory." He headed back to the living room, pulled the blinds back a slit with one finger and surveyed the street below.

Turning to look at her for the first time since they'd found her phone, he smiled. "Will you be okay here for a few minutes while I install the sensors?"

"Yeah. Go ahead." Her stomach roared to life again and not in a good way. Motion sensors, guns, on the run; it all held such surreal and negative vibes. She wouldn't be able to get used to a life like this.

He nodded, dug through his bag and pulled out a small

black case with, she assumed, the sensors. "Lock the door behind me, just in case."

Running her hands up and down her arms to ward off the chill that went through her, she opened the cabinets in hopes of finding coffee. Feeling lucky at her find of caramel and sea salt coffee, she set about brewing a pot. It would probably be a very long night. The mundane, routine task of finding cups and creamers and a spoon helped to settle her nerves. Fleetingly, she thought of calling Jolie to see how she was doing and let her know she was okay, but after the phone incident, she didn't want to screw anything up, so she set that thought aside.

The sound of voices floated up to her from below, and her heart hammered in her chest. Listening at the door for signs of friend or foe, she could only hear talking but not specific words. Sunflower may have guests, and hopefully, they were friendly, and no one knew they were here. Ford told her Rory gave their names as Michael and Jane, nothing suspicious or unusual enough to remember. The key to this apartment had been left in a lock box inside the garage, so they hadn't been seen.

A key inserted into the lock made her jump back, her heart pounding in her chest, her throat suddenly dry.

Ford stepped into the room, turned and locked the door and pulled his phone from his pocket. Bringing up the screen, he turned it toward her so she could see six green lights in tiny squares. "These are the sensors in the stairs at each entry point. They'll flash red if someone breaches a sensor. My phone will also chirp in case I'm not watching the screen."

He stepped up to her, and her heartbeat increased for a different reason this time. His strong arms enfolded her into a warm embrace and his head dipped to drop a kiss on the top of her head. "We'll be safe here tonight."

His firm warm body pressed tightly against hers soothed her in ways she never would have imagined. Just a simple hug from him made this situation feel so much better. It didn't hurt that he was handsome and had this security thing down like a boss.

"Do I smell coffee?"

Giggling, she replied, "Yes. Let me pour us a cup." Her heart felt lighter, at least a bit. She poured their coffees and carried them to the sofa where Ford sat with his laptop on his knees. "I thought you left that at the house?"

When his eyes met hers, butterflies swarmed her stomach, those dark depths so intense but so purely sexy. "I have an identical one at the house. This one stays in my truck."

"Wow, you *are* prepared, Ford." She chuckled and sat next to him, wanting to see what he was working on but not wanting to seem nosy.

"Yes, ma'am. Look here." He pointed to his computer which relieved her curiosity. "The house is secure, no one has tried to enter the land, and no one has stepped foot on my land. So, whatever the purpose of Tamra's phone call, to either root us out or to fish, so far, they seem to be leaving us alone. Rory and his guys are watching Stephano's house for activity, and I've not heard anything, so no news is good news."

He accepted the coffee cup from her hand and sipped at the warm brew. "Good. Thanks."

Placing his laptop on the wicker cube that served as a coffee table, he turned his head and locked eyes with her. "Tomorrow we're driving up to Margret June's cabin to see if Waylon and Bobby Ray are there. I'm not comfortable leaving you here alone, so I'm bringing you with me, but you'll need to stay in the truck. They can't see in, and you'll go unnoticed there. If they aren't there, then we'll swing by an apartment that's in the name of El Pablo Guzman."

He twisted to face her fully, his fingers tugging gently on the braid slung over her shoulder. "It's a long shot, but if they'd have the balls to hide out in the very apartment the cartel owns, we might get lucky. Let's hope they're arrogant enough to believe they can stay right under the noses of the very people they've stolen from."

Arrogant. Yep, they were that, all right. "Here's to arrogance." Raising her coffee cup in the air, she saluted and then sipped at her warm brew.

"Now, one last thing. Do you know how to handle and shoot a gun?"

CHAPTER 30

Driving toward the cabin, his stomach clenched tight. He'd woken up this morning with Megan nestled tightly to him, his arms holding her close, the fragrance of her hair, sweet and soft filling his senses. Now, he was bringing her here, and there could very well be danger. And, as stupid as it sounded, he was worried she'd see Waylon and feel something for him. He was afraid he'd see it in her face. They'd been driving for an hour and twenty minutes, and according to the GPS, they were almost there. He could feel it in his gut.

Sweat gathered between his shoulder blades—the first droplet skating down his spine at this moment. Turning the truck onto the gravel road, his heart hammered in his chest. His peripheral vision caught Megan's spine stiffen, and her breathing labored, her right hand holding her stomach. He'd shown her how to hold a gun this morning, how to remove the safety, and how to aim it should she need it, but they'd had no time to actually practice shooting. Hopefully, she wouldn't have to, and if she did, he hoped he wasn't in the way.

"Meg, remember, you stay in the truck, doors locked, and don't make a sound. Pick up the gun."

He glanced at her face, the clenching of her jaw evident. Her shoulders were so tight, they looked painful. He regretted bringing her along. She could have stayed with Emmy, but if he were honest, he was also a bit selfish where she was concerned. Hopefully not to the demise of either of them.

Megan slowly leaned forward and pulled the pistol from its holder bolted to the front of his console. Wrapping her fingers around the stock as he'd shown her, she kept it pointed at the floor, held between her knees, feet spread apart.

Pulling the truck to a stop, he surveyed the area at the end of the road. A shack stood to the left, woods to the right. No vehicles around, no tire tracks, and no life signs are visible. So, he'd have to go inside. Figured.

Backing his truck up and into the edge of the woods to, at a minimum, partially conceal it should someone else come looking down here and keep Megan as safe as possible, he put it in park, twisted to face her. "I'm leaving the keys in the ignition and the truck on, in case this goes bad, and a quick escape is needed. If you hear shots and don't see me running out of the shack or toward you, climb over the console and take off. Don't wait for me if they come for you. Hear me?"

"But, Ford, I ..."

"Megan. Honey. I need to know that whatever happens, you'll keep yourself safe." Moisture gathered in her eyes, and she swallowed hard, the sound loud in the quiet truck. "If you have to leave me here, you push this button right here as you start driving out. It'll connect you to Rory, who will call local authorities and send help. Promise me."

He framed her face with his hands, her eyes glassy but so very green in the sunlight that streamed in through the windshield. She'd pulled her curly auburn curls into a braid again this morning as he stood watching her deft fingers tame her wild mane. Her hair was becoming one of the features about her that appealed so very much to his imagination. Its softness was like nothing else he'd ever felt, its wildness intoxicating.

"I promise." She let out a deep breath. "But you need to promise me you'll try to come back to me. You'll be safe and do everything you can to come out here and leave with me."

He closed his eyes and touched his forehead to hers. His heart beat savagely in his chest. "I promise." His lips touched hers softly, which was just the opposite of what he wanted to do to her right now. Holding her tightly to him and never letting go would have been his preference.

"Okay. Ready?"

She let out a long breath. "Yeah."

Game face on. Scanning the area once again, he saw the footpath to the front of the cabin and decided he'd go in the opposite direction. If they were in there watching for intruders, they'd likely watch the footpath. He stepped from the truck and slowly pushed the door closed, motioned to Megan to lock the doors and once he heard the click, he pulled a gun from his waist holster, flicked the safety off and slowly made his way through the tall weeds to the back of the shack. Flies buzzed in the quiet, a squirrel scurried up the side of a tree, and he'd be lying if he said that didn't scare him just a smidge.

Reaching the back corner of the structure, he flattened his back to the building, looked across the distance to see his truck, the inside obscured by his window coating, but he knew she was watching him and scared. He nodded for her benefit, glanced around the landscape once more, peeked around the corner and edged his way along the wall to the back door. Taking a few deep breaths, he raised his gun, tried the door knob to find it open, opened it just a crack and listened for movement. When he heard nothing, he slid inside, keeping his back against the wall, and waited for his eyes to adjust to the darkened cabin, the only light streaming in between the tatters on the pathetic curtains still hanging in the windows.

Cobwebs strung here and there caught the sun's rays over the kitchen table. Dust coated heavily on the top had been disturbed by someone's hand swiping through it in a poor effort to clean a path. A bowl sat in the swath of cleared dust and a coffee cup alongside it. Moving silently, he touched the outside of the cup with the back of his forefinger. Cold. Milk rested in the bottom of the bowl—not curdled—the spoon resting there dry. Someone had been here this morning, or at the latest, yesterday afternoon. Glancing around the kitchen area, he saw that a cooler sat under a makeshift counter, which was nothing more than two by fours with a plywood top. The cooler wasn't dusty, though it was dirty. Lifting the top and peering inside, he found a quart of milk, a package of lunch meat, and a carton of eggs. Severely melted ice floated in the water along the bottom. It appeared someone was staying here. Stepping around the wall to what served as a living room, he saw a ratty sofa that looked like it had seen better days or possibly picked from the garbage and a rumpled sleeping bag on the top. Another sleeping bag lay wadded up in an old recliner, and the smell of the cabin became overwhelming—old blood and feces. Something silver peeked out from under the sleeping bag on the other side of the recliner. Inching forward, he picked it up, glanced at the amulet hanging from the chain and pocketed it.

The sound of a motor caught his attention and he knew he'd either need to get out or stay and surprise them and since his mission was to capture Bobby Ray June, he flattened his back to the darkness in the corner and hoped like hell he would have the element of surprise in his favor.

As the motor grew louder, the distinct sound of a four-wheeler explained why there wasn't a vehicle around and why tire tracks weren't visible. They likely hid their truck or car—whatever they were using for transportation in the woods—and used the four-wheeler to travel to and from.

The motor slowed, and he held his breath, hoping they hadn't noticed the truck. The low murmur of the stilled four-wheeler filled the air, followed by low voices. Then the four-wheeler engine raced and sounded as it slowly became softer the farther away it went. Staying in place for a few moments, waiting to see if one of them had stayed behind, he worked to slow his breathing. Twisting his neck, he looked around the corner to the kitchen area and saw no signs of movement, heard no sounds. Braving a step into the room, he glanced out the window, scanning as much of the area as he could see and saw nothing and no one move. Exiting the shack, he looked across the weeds to see his truck, undisturbed. Slowly making his way back to his truck, he kept his eyes vigilant. Nothing. Not a sound.

As his hand gripped the door handle, he heard the locks click, and in one swift movement, he hoisted himself into the truck, pleased when Megan locked the doors the second he closed his door.

CHAPTER 31

"Oh my God. I've never been so scared in my life. I'm not kidding. Fucking scared." She was thrilled to see him, whole and alive, but her heart pounded hard in her chest, and she was grateful for good health right now that she could sustain this kind of excitement.

"Was it them on the four-wheeler? Did they both leave, and which way did they go?"

He looked into her eyes, and scary Ford was back. "Yes, both of them, and they went through the woods in that direction. They saw me. The truck. Fuck, I was scared."

His grin spread on his face, and it was beautiful. "You're beginning to talk like a sailor, or at the very least, my sister."

"I'm sorry. My grandma would be so pissed that I used it. But I don't have words to describe how scared I was." Her breaths came in bursts.

He reached for her head and pulled her close, kissing her forehead, then her lips. "I'm so sorry, Megan. Hang tough with me, okay?"

Quickly nodding, she vowed to herself that she could do this and be tough. He didn't need to be distracted by her. He kissed her forehead again and put the truck in drive. Easing the truck down the gravel road, his eyes always scanning for movement, she marveled at his strength and courage. He was admirable in so many ways.

She began scanning the horizon as well, looking for any signs of life or danger or movement.

"Do you know what kind of vehicle either of them might have?"

"No. I honestly haven't seen Waylon in years, since we divorced, so about five years now. Bobby Ray, I never paid any attention to him."

She watched his jaw work, just the mere mention of Bobby Ray did something to him. Understandable, for sure.

"Margret June died a few years ago. Their daddies were brothers and very close. Waylon is an only child, so he stuck close to Bobby Ray. Bobby Ray has a sister who lives in Texas now, I think."

"That's what my file says." His jaw clenched then relaxed. She assumed by great effort.

Of course, he'd have a file. He'd been researching Bobby Ray for years. She took in a deep breath; she didn't need to know, but ... "Am I in your file?"

He turned his head and captured her gaze. The action always made her body do funny things. Her heart always hitched up a few beats, her panties always dampened, and she always flushed. She could feel the burning in her chest at this very moment. Remembering his strong work roughened hands on her hips, all over her body, made her squirm in her seat.

"Yes. It's how I found you."

"What does it say?" She took a deep breath. "About me. What does it say? Am I bad or good?"

His right hand grabbed her left hand and held it tight.

"My file doesn't judge or determine bad or good, Meg. It's just the basics. Where you worked. When you divorced. Your address, those things. I'll let you read it tonight when we stop, if it'll make you feel better."

She swallowed. "We'll see." Quickly glancing at his face, her lips trembled into a smile. "Maybe."

That seemed to work for him because he squeezed her hand again, then put his hand back on the steering wheel. Once again searching for his prey.

Reaching the county road, Ford turned slowly onto it in the direction that Waylon and Bobby Ray had traveled— slowly traveling along the road, looking into the woods for any signs of movement. Once they'd passed the wooded area and came to a corner, he sped up and headed toward South Pass.

"Waylon have any kind of a man cave at the house? In the garage or basement?"

"No. My grandpa had a work room in the basement. He used to make birdhouses and little wooden decorations. Waylon would go down there sometimes, but he didn't make anything. I guess he just needed a quiet place to think."

"And you never felt like he came back to the house after you divorced?"

Shaking her head, her brows pinched together. Had she? God, she was a moron. "I don't think so. I don't know. Why would he?"

"I don't know. Just piecing things together."

The first thing she was going to do when she could get back in her house is go to the basement and see if something was there. Sitting here and thinking about it now, she didn't always lock her doors. South Pass was safe, or so she thought. The ringing of his phone broke into her thoughts.

"Montgomery." His Bluetooth engaged.

"Marcus is on his way to South Pass. He's about forty-five minutes out."

"Thanks, Rory. I found the shack; they're staying there, or they were. They saw my truck and took off on a four-wheeler into the woods. If they think they've been found, they'll be moving again."

"Okay. We'll be watching Marcus. No idea if he knows you're there or if he has orders to find Waylon, but I have two patrols watching Stephano's house, and I'll have locals watching Marcus."

"Thanks, Rory. Any word from the fire department on Megan's house? We'd like to get in there if we can."

This was news. Good news. Maybe. She watched his profile as he drove. Classic nose, dark brows over those impossibly dark eyes. His coal black hair reflected the sunlight as a mirror would. A few silver strands above his ears glinted in the sun. How had she not noticed those before? It gave him that silver fox appeal, not that he needed more than he already had. What on earth was wrong with Tamra to let him go? To intentionally push him away?

"I'll call you back with word. I haven't heard from the chief today at all."

"Okay. Thanks."

A click sounded, and the call ended. "There's never any banter with you two. Are you friends outside of work?"

"Of course. We served together. We're brothers—battle brothers."

"But it's always so ... ah, clinical or something when you talk."

"Lately, when we talk, it's about work. When we talk outside of work, it's different. We have dangerous jobs, and we need our attention focused on the task at hand."

"Okay." Made sense. When she and Jolie talked on the phone, it could go on and on for an hour or more. They always had so much to say while actually saying nothing. She'd have to see if Ford would let her stop by to see her friend. She must be worried sick.

"Still have that burner phone I gave you?"

"Yeah."

"Pull up an Airbnb in South Pass for tonight. I don't want to stay in the same place."

Okay, that was good, it would keep her busy for a bit, and maybe her stomach would settle.

Finding a place she thought would work out—on Main Street, easy to see the area and easy for the police to patrol, she told Ford about it. He leaned forward and pulled his wallet from his back pocket. "Use the Visa."

Just as she finished booking their room, Ford's phone rang once again.

"Montgomery."

"No go on the house, Ford. Chief says maybe later. They're in there right now finishing up the investigation."

"Roger. Thanks." He turned to face her. "I'm going to have to go ask a few questions of some of the patrons at The Bullseye. I understand that's where Waylon hung out. I hate to bring you in there. It's not the place I'd ever want my woman to venture into. That said, do you think your friend Jolie is home for a short visit?"

Now this sounded good. He called her "my woman" which was exciting in a caveman sort of way, and she was going to see Jolie.

"My woman?" She had to give him a little grief.

"You don't think you're my woman?"

Wow. Her heart started its racing again for about the

tenth time today, but this time it felt awesome. "I guess I hadn't thought about it."

He chuckled and turned down Second Street on the edge of town that would bring them close to Jolie's house.

Needing to lighten the suddenly serious vibe that just entered the truck, she responded to his earlier question. "She's a stay-at-home mom; she'll be home."

"Meg? You can't tell her where we're staying. No one, not even Jolie, can know. I won't even tell Emmy or Dawson. Okay?"

"I promise." She smiled at him. It probably looked like beaming, but after the scare she'd had at the shack, the news of visiting Jolie was welcome. Plus, once the fear had left her, she had to admit it was sort of exciting riding along with Ford. Maybe she'd become a badass one day, and Jolie could help her come up with a badass bounty hunter name.

CHAPTER 32

Seeing Megan to the door at Jolie's, he kissed her lips, more than once, then tipped his head to Jolie and sauntered to his truck rather proud of himself. After all, when he said he wouldn't want to bring his woman to a bar like The Bullseye, he wasn't referencing Megan in particular, but he meant anyone he cared about. But the instant it was out of his mouth, he realized he wanted her to be his woman. He wanted her to want to be his woman. If only he weren't still married and things were different.

He pulled to the curb outside of the seedy looking bar. Even the street it was on looked like the back end of the town. Dingy buildings lined the street—some of them not even straight—looking like a good strong wind would topple them over in a heartbeat.

The front door was held open with a barstool. The only two windows in front held dirty, bug-crusted neon signs, and both were cracked. The sign hanging over the front door was a beer sign; the plastic insert that no doubt had the bar's name painted on it had long been gone. So the dim light bulb inside was visible.

Once he shut his truck off, the music from the jukebox rolled out into the street, the current tune an old country ballad by Conway Twitty. The music playing inside was as old as the bar itself. Entering the dark, dank building, the smell of stale beer and old cigarette smoke assaulted his nostrils. His feet made noise as he walked deeper into the bar, as his shoes stuck in the layers of spilled substances from years gone by and popped when he pulled them up to take a step.

Locating a space somewhere close to the middle of the bar, he plopped on the stool, trying to blend in as much as possible, but since he'd recently showered and shaved, it was nearly impossible. A quick glance down the bar showed the general population here drank tap beer. Shit.

"What'll it be, buddy?" asked the bartender. His dirty wife beater stretched across a beer belly and didn't quite meet its goal to cover the large pasty expanse that hung under it.

"Tap beer. The Olds is good." Reaching into his pocket, he pulled a five dollar bill out and tossed it on the bar. No need in looking like he had money in a place like this. He'd sit here a bit and see if anyone engaged him in conversation.

As he drank his beer, his ears tuned into a conversation at the end of the bar, toward the bathrooms in the back.

"You get your new stuff yet?" a younger man with a Pittsburgh Steelers hat on said to the man next to him, sporting an oversized cowboy hat on his greasy head.

"Naw. He's supposed to meet me later out back."

"'Kay. I'll be here too. I needed some cash this week and got some leads to make scores."

"Give 'im a coupla hours."

They were trying to talk softly, but the amount of alcohol it looked like they'd already consumed made it impossible. No one else in the bar seemed to pay them any mind so it must just be business as usual. He continued sipping his beer hoping to hear who this would-be dealer was. It would just be too perfect that he would find Waylon like this.

The stool next to him pulled away from the bar, and a large man around six feet six stood where the stool had once been. The man looked as out of place as he felt. Aftershave floated over the other odors in the bar, and as he took a better look at the man, he could see his clothing was of better quality than anyone else here in the bar. Long sleeves rolled back to the elbow of a blue dress shirt, tucked into black jeans and the man wore cowboy boots which peaked out from under his pants. When he looked up into the man's face, he found he was being watched by this big man, and his stomach knotted. Keeping it cool, he asked, "Can I buy you a drink, mister?"

"You don't look like you belong in here."

"I was thinking the same about you."

The man chuckled, then held out his hand. "Name's Bull and I own this dump."

Shaking hands with Bull, he replied, "Ford. Nice place."

Bull threw his head back and laughed. "Naw, it ain't, but you wouldn't believe the cash that rolls through this place."

"Shorty, get my friend Ford here a beer and bring me a scotch."

The fat man behind the bar waddled to the back bar and poured a top shelf scotch into a glass. Setting it in front of Bull, he grabbed Ford's empty glass and refilled it with the tap beer he'd previously drank. Setting it in front of him, Shorty cranked his head back and looked up at his employer. "Anything else, boss?"

"Any word from our friend?"

Shorty nodded to the two men at the end of the bar. "Jason and Welch are meeting him a bit later."

Bull looked at the two men, his lip slightly curled up. Picking up his glass, he downed a large majority of the drink without missing a beat. The first thing that came to mind was one tough son of a bitch. He'd never be able to down that much scotch without his eyes watering.

"What brings you here, Ford?"

"Needed a drink. Old lady ragging on me. I'm new in town, dropped her off at her sister's and came here to hide."

Bull slapped him on the back with one of his big paws and guffawed as if he'd been there before.

"Poor son of a bitch."

Nodding his head in agreement, he began thinking he'd struck gold here. This shithole made money because they were selling drugs from it. He'd bet his left nut that this was Waylon's connection. As soon as he could, he'd get Rory looking into The Bullseye.

Picking up his scotch, Bull slapped him on the back once more. "Nice meeting ya, Ford."

He sauntered past the two men at the end of the bar, around a corner and disappeared from sight. Playing it cool, Ford finished his beer then hefted himself off his stool. With a slight wave to the bartender, he exited the bar pleased for the fresh air to fill his lungs. He felt like he needed a shower.

Climbing into his truck, he pulled away from the curb but made it a point to look behind the bar to see some men gathering at the back door, loading boxes into the back of a pickup truck.

Tapping his phone, he dialed up Rory.

"Yeah."

"I need you to do a bit of research on a dump called The Bullseye. I have a big hunch that's Waylon's connection in town for selling drugs. I may also need backup. They're expecting someone with some stuff in about an hour."

CHAPTER 33

Her visit with Jolie was awesome but cut a bit short when her friend had to leave to pick up her daughter, Sally Ann, from dance lessons. Jolie offered to bring her along, but Megan asked to be dropped off at her house instead. She needed to get inside and see if she could find her grandma's necklace and she'd like to take the opportunity to gather a few more clothes.

"Ah, no. I'm not dropping you off there. Are you crazy? They'd look for you there for sure, Megan."

"I'll be quiet and sneak in and then out. I've just got to see it, Jolie."

"Didn't you say that Ford would take you there once the chief said it was okay?"

Her shoulders sank, she had said that.

"Fine. Will you take me to the Log Cabin then, so I can check in with Nila? I'll call Ford and tell him to pick me up there, and I promise, I'll stay in the back."

The nicest thing she'd learned was Jolie's husband, Derek, boarded up her front window and fixed her door. Now armed with a new key, she'd simply let herself in and stay close to the walls in case the floor wasn't safe. She also wanted to check out the basement and see if Waylon had been using her house for nefarious purposes.

A few minutes later, she stood at the back door of the Log Cabin, the aroma of freshly baked pies and bacon floating out to greet her made her stomach growl. Knowing full well she should do as she said she would, she turned instead to begin walking the three blocks to her house. She could stay out of sight by walking through the yards of her neighbors. In the summer when it was nice, there were days she'd make the walk, enjoying the quiet little town for what it was, a quiet little town. Today, for some reason it didn't feel that way.

Skittering across Joseph Street, she felt like everyone in town was watching her from behind their curtains. Her shoulders were stiff, and she felt like she was walking in slow motion, unable to make any time at all.

Hearing Mrs. Baxter yell from her porch, "Hey! Get off there."

She spun around to see two neighborhood kids jumping on a stump in her front yard, but it was enough of a heart starter that she quickened her pace. Finally reaching the yard directly behind hers, she scooted along the hedgerow, ducking down, so her head was below the top of the hedges. That probably didn't look suspicious at all, but she managed to make it to the front of her house, without anyone noticing her.

So here she stood on her sweet front porch, and it looked totally different than it had the last time she stood here admiring her little house. That same dreaded feeling hit her stomach as she looked at her home, blackened and taped with crime scene tape. Her front window was now a piece of plywood, the front door no longer hanging precariously on one hinge and a shiny new lock the only clean place on the house. It looked sad and unlivable. It also looked terribly small next to Ford's home. A flush of embarrassment raced through her body at what he must think about her little home. But she'd done the best she could, and her grandmother loved that house all the same. So did she. Now, though, after all they'd been through, she didn't feel safe here anymore. Marcus had most likely been able to get inside, while she had been in there no less, and now she wondered if Waylon had been inside too. Older houses often had older locks, which were easy to jimmy. And admittedly, when you didn't lock up your house, it was open for anyone to enter. She'd never do that again.

Blowing out a breath, she looked up and down both sides of the street. The investigation crew was nowhere in sight, and the street was empty. Settling the key into the new lock, she turned it to the right, and the door popped right open. Quickly stepping inside, she closed it behind her, turning the lock for good measure.

The stale stench of burnt paint and furniture, glues, and insulation stung her nose. This wasn't like a nice camp fire; it was gross. The blackened walls looked pitiful, and her eyes watered. She hadn't really allowed herself a good cry over all that she'd lost, but that could wait for the right moment. Honestly, her head struggled to wrap itself around everything that she'd been through because things kept happening before she could process them. Then Ford. He happened and changed her whole life. She'd been content to just live alone and serve Nila's food. Once in a while, she thought about buying the diner from her when she retired, but that seemed a way off. Now, that probably wouldn't settle her soul anymore. Ford showed her a new life. She felt beautiful in his arms, the way he looked at her. She felt needed and smart and funny when she made him laugh. She'd never missed it before because she'd never had it. In retrospect, her relationship with Waylon had been more brother/sister in a way.

Shaking her head to wake herself up, she inched her way toward her bedroom. Ford hadn't given her any indication that there'd be more for them once he found Bobby Ray and her house situation was taken care of. He had called her his woman, but that was joking around.

Her bedroom hadn't suffered as much as the living room, and she felt safer walking around in here. Though everything smelled of smoke, as she recalled from bringing her clothes to Ford's. Checking the bedside table where she kept her necklace, she looked under the table, under the bed, all around the room. Nothing. It made no sense.

Going into her closet, she began pulling clothing out she wanted to take with her, so she had more than just two pairs of jeans and two T-shirts. Remembering her flat iron, she made a mental note to stop in her bathroom to grab that and a few other feminine necessities. She'd need them in about a week. Searching around for one of her tote bags, she dug around in the back of the closet. The one thing her grandmother had done about five years before she died was to enlarge the tiny closet that had been in this room and made this lovely walk-in. Reaching up on a higher shelf, she found the bag she wanted. That's when she heard it.

The back door opened then closed. It always had that darn squeak in it. She froze, her heart racing so loud in her ears she couldn't hear anything else. She closed her eyes and focused on slowing her breathing. Careful not to make any noise, she inched her way toward the closet door and listened. Someone went into the basement, their feet thumping along on the old wooden steps. They weren't even trying to be quiet. Skirting the squeaky floorboard in front of the closet door, she inched her way across the floor. Gripping her tote bag tightly, she placed a hand over her stomach to keep it from rolling.

Now standing in front of the heat vent in her bedroom, she could hear the person in the basement, boxes sliding across the floor. A grunt sounded. The boxes must be heavy. She didn't have anything down there that was heavy and in a box. She didn't have much down there other than Christmas decorations and a few planters she hadn't used this year. No telling what condition any of that was in now. The back door opened and closed again, and her heart pounded. Someone else had entered the kitchen. She could still hear the person in the basement. Oh my God. Glancing toward the window, she didn't think she could climb out of it without making noise. Turning to look at the bedroom door, she thought about closing and locking it, but if someone was here to burn her damned house down again, she'd be trapped. Though she wouldn't care if she made noise then.

Slow, methodical footsteps sounded in the kitchen, someone walking around trying to be quiet, but she was so tuned in now she'd hear every peep. Grunting sounded from the basement again, then she heard him, "Christ, this is heavy."

For chrissake, that was Waylon's voice.

CHAPTER 34

Parking his truck down the street, he walked along the edge of the garage, looked in the window to see Megan's Jeep still inside and then saw one Waylon June running across the back yard from the street at the back of the house. Running wasn't really the term for it, he was simply too large to run, maybe lopping was a better word for it. At any rate, he watched from the side of the garage as Waylon used a key on the back door, opened it up, and stepped inside.

Now if he were a betting man, he'd bet that piece of shit had been hiding those stolen drugs in Megan's basement all along. Once Waylon was inside, he inched his way across the back lawn to the door Waylon had disappeared through. Stepping up to the door, he glanced in through the window and saw the basement door, directly in front of the back door, was opened and the lights were on.

Taking a chance that the door was unlocked, he quietly turned the knob and smiled when it unlatched for him. Stepping into the house, he closed the back door and inched his way along the kitchen wall, out of sight of the basement door so he'd have the element of surprise. Unholstering his gun, he flicked the safety and held it at chest height. Hearing Waylon grunt and swear in the basement was comical. The man clearly wasn't used to a hard day's work. Glancing across the kitchen, he saw the point of origin of the fire directly in front of the stove—a deeply blackened circle on the floor, and the hole almost all the way through the flooring to the basement below. It spread out from there and raced across the floor. Another blackened circle stood next to the kitchen table on the floor, and that was where the explosion must have happened. The wall between the kitchen and living room had blown apart but thank goodness it had been there. It was likely what saved Megan. It also didn't look like Bobby Ray's work. When he set fires, he lit little fires all around the house after dumping gasoline throughout to make sure everything caught. This actually looked accidental.

Hearing Waylon's heavy footsteps on the wooden stairs, he flattened his back against the wall. His heart hammered; it always did just before apprehension. Calming himself with his breathing, he inhaled and exhaled slowly twice as he listened to Waylon slowly approaching. As he reached the top step and side stepped to open the back door, Ford kicked him hard at the back of his knees, causing them both to buckle. The heavy box Waylon carried hit him in the shoulder, making him cry out, then it hit the floor and broke open. Working quickly while Waylon was still unaware, Ford reached forward and secured both of Waylon's wrists in the zip ties he always carried. Dragging him away from the door across the black floor by the feet, Waylon began swearing and sputtering.

"Fucking asshole. Let me go."

Ignoring him to survey the contents of the box he carried, he saw cans of coffee, one spilled open to reveal baggies of what was most likely cocaine amid the mess of coffee grounds strewn about.

"Well, what do we have here, Waylon? Stolen drugs, I'll bet." He trained his gun on Waylon's head.

"You don't know a fucking thing, asshole."

Ford stood and pulled his phone from his back pocket.

"I'll tell you what I do know. Marcus and Stephano would love their drugs back."

He tapped an icon on his phone, watching Waylon intently.

"Yeah."

"Can you patch me through to Stephano?"

"Ford, are you sure this is a good idea?"

"Yep. Patch me through."

It didn't go unnoticed that Waylon's eyes grew three sizes in his dirty head. His scuffled hair long ago in need of a cut and some shampoo was now blackened from falling on the floor and littered with coffee grounds.

"Please don't tell him. He'll kill me. Just let me go, and I promise I'll leave the US and never return."

Chuckling, he listened as a series of clicks sounded on his phone then he heard Stephano's voice for the first time in the ten years since Tamra moved in with him. His stomach turned at what this monster had done to her. Supplying her with just enough drugs to keep her happy but not so much that she'd kill herself.

"I have something you want."

"I'm listening."

"I want a deal first."

A chuckle sounded on the other side of the phone. "A deal? What could you possibly want from me to deal?"

"I have your drugs and your thief. You have my wife, and I'd like her to be my *ex*-wife. You make that happen, you'll get what you want."

Silence. He didn't even know where that came from. It was against everything he'd ever known to bargain with a drug smuggler. And in truth, he'd be handing Waylon and the drugs over to the cops as soon as they got here. But he thought it was worth a shot.

"Well now, let's see, you want to give me a thief and in return, I should give you a divorce from a cokehead. It doesn't really seem fair to me, Ford."

"Okay. I'll just give it all to the cops. They should be here any moment now."

He tapped his end call button and waited. His stomach in knots, his heart pounding.

"Ford. What are you doing?"

He swung his head around to see Megan, eyes wide, skin pale, and she was looking at Waylon. Not him. Waylon. He'd just tried to make a deal with a smuggler for her, and she was concerned about her piece of shit ex-husband. What the fuck was wrong with him? He seriously had to swear off of women.

"Get out of here, Megan."

"What are you doing? You can't shoot him. You've got handcuffs on him. That's not right."

"Get out, Megan."

"No." She stepped closer. "Waylon, tell me what's going on here."

"Make him put the gun away."

She stopped forward progress and crossed her arms over

her chest. "You tell me right now what you've been doing here."

Waylon dropped his head to the floor. "Goddammit, you are the most stubborn piece of ass ever in the fucking world."

Her eyes narrowed. "Did you set my house on fire?" She bent slightly toward him. "Were you storing drugs in my basement?"

"Goooooooood, I'm so sick of you and your pious bullshit. We could have had a great life. But nooooo, you were too good for me. Fucking cunt."

Megan walked closer to Waylon and kicked him so hard, he howled. "You piece of shit," she spat.

She looked up at him then, her eyes that bright green he'd fallen in love with. "Shoot him, Ford."

His head spun. Must be the left-over fumes in the house. He was in love with her? Aww, shit.

"I'll take care of that." Marcus stepped into the kitchen, gun drawn. "This is my problem right now. I'll take care of Waylon."

"Don't shoot him. I need to know where Bobby Ray is." He glanced down at Waylon. "Where is he? Where are you two staying?"

"Fuck you."

Bang! A shot rang out. Megan screamed and jumped back, and Waylon howled. A red circlet formed on his thigh where Marcus had shot him. "I've got another one for you."

"No. No. Don't shoot. I'll tell."

Ford signaled to Megan to come closer, the look on her face sheer terror now. Her legs looked wobbly as if she'd collapse at any moment, so he inched closer to her and pulled her into his arms. Edging back toward the wall, her shaking body against his was both a balm and a wound. She never took her eyes from Waylon, her arms circling her waist. He held her close with one arm, the other still holding his gun.

"He's at The Bullseye." He dropped his head. "Fuck."

CHAPTER 35

Never in her life had she seen someone shot. Not that it was a mortal wound, but still, she was staring at her ex-husband laying on the dirty floor, hands tied behind his back and a bloodied leg where he'd just been shot. She didn't have feelings for him anymore, but she wanted answers. For some damned reason, over the past few years, there had been times when she worried that she hadn't tried hard enough to make their marriage work. Hearing once again how he'd been screwing her over would seal that thought behind a brick wall and keep it there.

"Speak up, Waylon, tell me what you've been doing here."

He twisted his head back to stare at her, his lips curled back in a snarl. "Fuck, Megan. The fire was an accident. I got ahold of a rock of meth, and I was trying it out here. I heard you come home after I lit the pipe. I froze trying not to make a sound, and when you went into the bedroom, I was going to leave. The fucking pipe caught on fire then, and you walked out of the bedroom. I dropped the fucking pipe, and it started that stupid ugly rug you had in front of the stove on fire. I took off running. I didn't know there would be an explosion."

She kicked at his leg, just below his wound, with the toe of her tennis shoe. "Why were you here, Waylon?" She was trying to keep her voice neutral. Yelling at him never did a damned thing.

"Fuck, isn't it obvious? Geez, you're stupid."

"I want to hear you say it." She nudged him in the leg again.

"Ouch. Stop that." He tried scooting away, but Marcus stepped on his back to halt his progress. "Shit. All right. Fuck. Bobby Ray needed money. I figured I could take some drugs and we could sell them quickly and get out of town. We needed more money than I thought to bribe that fucking transport asshole. Then everyone was looking for us, so we had to hide out."

Marcus put pressure on his back, and Waylon groaned as his face was pressed to the floor.

"Those my drugs, asshole?"

"Yes," Waylon cried out as Marcus put his foot on his shot leg. "Ow!" he cried.

Marcus pulled his phone out of his pocket, but Ford interrupted him. "No, you don't. Bobby Ray is mine!"

"He's the reason my drugs were stolen."

Ford removed his arm from around her shoulders, and she immediately felt the loss of his strength. "I can trump that. He's the reason my parents are dead."

The two men stared at each other for a long time—so long her heart began racing, her palms dampened and the hairs on the back of her neck rose. Ford could look scary, just like he did right now, but Marcus could rival that scary. His eyes almost as black as Ford's, his short, cropped dark hair and devilish looking goatee coming to a point looked positively evil.

Swallowing, she thought she'd try to change the standoff. "Um. Please. Can we just go?"

Waylon twisted his body. "You can't leave me here with him, he'll kill me."

So sick of his whining and bullshit, she'd had enough. "I'd like to kill you myself, right now." Stepping forward toward him she pointed to her chest. "You could have gotten me in a lot of trouble, Waylon. This ..." She pointed at Marcus. "... man was harassing me. He snuck into this house and put a tracking device on my fucking phone. I had drugs here; the cops could have searched my house and found them. I don't care what happens to you."

She kicked him again for good measure. Scared. Mad. Fed up. And a little nauseous, all she wanted was to get out of here and soon. Before she and Ford were killed too. She didn't doubt he'd do what he could to protect her, but she didn't want him stepping in front of a bullet for her. "Ford, can we just go?"

He was still staring at Marcus, both of them relentless in their determination. "Tell you what," Marcus began. "You can leave here. Stephano said you two had an agreement. I keep Waylon and the drugs, and you go get Bobby Ray. We don't really give a shit about him. You never saw me here. You don't know a damned thing."

Ford's jaw clenched several times, and she was worried he'd say no. "You leave Megan alone."

A creepy smirk slid across Marcus' face, then a beat later, a slight incline of his head. Hopefully, that was a yes.

Softly, she wrapped her fingers around the crook of his arm at the elbow and tugged. "Please, Ford. Let's go."

Almost imperceptible, he nodded and stepped back but

kept his gun leveled on Marcus. "Megan, go to the front door."

"Ford."

"Go, I'm right behind you, but I'm not turning my back on this asshole."

Marcus smiled. Or sneered. It was hard to tell.

She glanced quickly at Waylon, probably the last time she'd see him. He would either go to jail, or ... well, she wouldn't think of the other. Nothing she'd be able to do about it now. he'd basically dug his own grave.

Slowly, she edged the kitchen, kind of afraid to turn her back on Marcus too. "Don't leave me here," Waylon hollered.

She kept backing away, trying not to touch the walls. Once she moved into the living room, she ran back to her bedroom and grabbed the bag she'd packed. As she exited the bedroom, Ford had backed into the living room, and she quickly opened the door and stepped outside. Taking a deep breath of clean air, she kept her feet moving to the edge of her yard. Sirens came into her hearing range, and she hoped they were on their way here. Ford caught up with her and steered her in the opposite direction, down the street. She looked up and saw his truck several houses down the street.

"Get cops to The Bullseye, Bobby Ray is there. A full search if you can't see him readily."

A brief glance showed her he was on his phone again, probably with Rory. Maybe this whole nightmare would be over. Finally. Doubtful she'd ever feel safe anywhere again, but she was looking forward to not seeing Marcus at every turn. Hopefully.

Her knees felt like rubber, and she worried they'd buckle before they reached Ford's truck. As if he could read her thoughts, he picked her up as if she were a feather and carried her the rest of the way. Looking up into his face, all she saw was determination.

Reaching the truck, he fished for his keys without setting her down, popped the locks, opened the door, and gently set her inside. "Buckle up," was all he said as he raced around the truck to the driver's side. That's when she heard a gunshot ring out.

CHAPTER 36

It was almost over. He'd be able to rest easier now knowing Bobby Ray was brought to justice. No way in hell Bobby would ever have a moment's peace again, and there was no way he'd ever be able to escape again. Security would damned near be up his ass.

A shot rang out just as he opened the driver's door. He paused, then quickly jumped into the truck. As he turned the key in the ignition, he turned to look at Megan. She sat staring at her house, no readable emotion on her face. She sat stock still as if she were waiting for someone to walk out of the front door. "Hey. You okay?"

Turning her stunning face to his, a soft smile shaped her lips. "I'm fine. We should go."

"Meg. That was probably ..."

"I know."

Nodding, he put the truck in gear and headed over to The Bullseye, hoping to see it swarming with cops.

Small towns were mostly the same. Everyone knew everyone's business, and when something big happened in town, word got around fast. This was the case today. Pulling up to The Bullseye, the number of people and cars in this part of town was probably triple to what it normally was, which wasn't saying a lot; not many people came down here on your average day. Two police cars, an ambulance, and about fifty people milled about the street, everyone trying to get a look at what was going on inside the seedy little bar at the end of the street. One of the cops was setting up wooden barricades, which wouldn't hold anyone back, but would keep the honest back. Hopefully.

Reaching over, he squeezed her hand. "Hey, I have to go and see what's going on and make sure I get my collar."

Green eyes sought his, her brows slightly furrowed. "Collar?"

"Baby, Bobby Ray is mine. And, the reward doesn't mean that much to me, but it'll help for the foundation, and I want to make sure that piece of shit is off the street."

She twisted in the seat now and looked at him straight on. Her brows raised into her hairline. "Foundation?"

Chuckling, he answered her, "Emmy and I started a foundation for kids affected by violence. We've both seen way too many in our time."

"Wow." She leaned forward, palming his cheek with her right hand. "You're something, Ford Montgomery."

He kissed her nose. "Anyway, please stay here, so you stay safe."

"No. I want to go and see for myself. I want him to see my face when they shove him in the back of a cop car."

"Meg."

"Nope. I deserve this too. You do more, but so do I."

Before he could say another word, she'd opened her door and jumped from the truck. The grin she bestowed on him through the window was pure insolence and sexy. Quickly following her, he stepped down from the vehicle and took her hand in his as he walked them toward the nearest cop. Pulling his ID from his pocket, he showed it to the young cop setting up the barricade. He looked them both over and shook his head. "You'll both need flak jackets to get any closer."

"Stay here," he mumbled to her. Jogging back to his truck, he opened the tailgate and pulled two flak jackets from the carrier bolted to the inside of his truck. He pulled his on as he made his way back to Megan.

Holding it open for her to slide her arms through, he kissed the top of her head as he affixed the Velcro closures, securing it tightly. Glancing at the cop, he got the go ahead nod and taking her hand once again, he pulled her to the cop car nearest the bar. An officer standing next to the car glanced their way, and he flashed his ID once again. "This is your collar? Chief told me to expect you."

"Yes, sir." He glanced toward the bar. "What have you found so far?"

"Nothing." He surveyed the area once again then stopped at the front of the bar. "Yet."

"Dammit." If Bobby Ray was here, he shouldn't be that hard to find. So, either he'd gotten wind of them coming here and took off, or he had a great hiding place. Or, he was being hidden. That was the likely scenario. "I'm going in."

"You can. She can't." The bored looking cop said.

"It's okay. Go. I'll be right here."

Kissing her quickly, he walked to the front door of the bar, held up his ID to the cop inside the door and glanced around the room. Everyone had been cleared from the bar except Bull, who sat looking extremely pissed off at a beat up wooden table in the corner as he was interviewed by another officer. Their eyes met, and Bull's narrowed. He'd be lying if he said that didn't scare him just a bit. Bull was massive and could probably tear him apart in a nanosecond, so he'd hope they could find Bobby Ray before Bull completely lost it. Walking farther into the bar and down the back hall he'd seen Bull disappear into earlier, he stepped through a door to what appeared to be an office. A large desk sat against the wall littered with papers and debris, a couple dirty glasses and a computer. A young blond man sat at the computer, trying to hack into Bull's system. His fingers brushed over the keys with lightning speed, but he seemed to be struggling a bit.

Leaving him to his work and glancing around the office, he began sifting through papers lying here and there, but nothing seemed to lead him to any drugs or Bobby Ray. Of course, they usually made their deals on the sly. Turning to survey the entire room, he noticed an ugly ass painting of Bull, life sized at that, against the wall next to the desk. On the other side of that stood a metal file cabinet. With the door open, the file cabinet was hidden. The wall next to the door held an old orange sofa, worn with an ass dent in the far end cushion, clearly where Bull spent most of his time here.

Ducking out of the room, he wandered farther down the hall to another room where an officer was moving cases of booze away from the wall looking for a secret passageway.

"This place have a basement?"

"No, sir. We weren't able to find one."

Taking a closer look at the walls, they looked solid. He rapped his knuckles against the outside wall, and the hollow sound raised his eyebrows. The dark-haired officer moving boxes—his badge said James—stopped and stared at him, his brow raised as well.

Rapping on the wall again in a different spot, it again sounded hollow. Officer James held up a finger and stepped out of the room. Ford followed him to the back door where they both exited and turned to examine the building. From where they stood, estimating the depth of the room, it appeared there was an additional narrow room built on to the outside of the building. The officer walked around to the side and came back. "No door."

Tilting his head up to see if there was a second level or window, they saw nothing but siding.

Heading back to the room, he examined the wall that he'd originally thought was an outside wall. Pushing on the wall to see if it moved, they were both disappointed to find nothing budged, not even a small flex.

Walking back to the office, which was just the next room down, he began tapping on the wall. The officer followed him and started moving chairs away from the wall.

"Hang on, James. So, if there were a false wall, it would be for a purpose. So, entry and exit would have to be easy to get to but still hidden. Where is that here?"

Craning their necks to look the room over, nothing stuck out. His eyes landed on that ugly ass picture of Bull, and he walked over to it. It seemed affixed to the wall solidly. Placing his hands on either side of the painting, he rocked it back and forth and after a loud click, it slid to the side, revealing a hallway that headed toward the outside of the building.

Officer James stepped forward, gun in hand and peered around the newly found doorway. Finding the passageway empty, he stepped inside. His gun out, he nodded to Officer James and followed him into the cramped space. Taking three steps toward the back of the passageway, a sound rang out, as if someone burst through a door, letting it bang closed. Screaming erupted outside.

CHAPTER 37

Her heart hammered in her chest; this was nerve wracking. The only thing that made it bearable was that it didn't seem like anything of interest was going on. Other than the people standing around, mostly behind her, thanks to Ford getting her past the barricade, chatting and guessing what was going on. From what she could overhear, the majority of her fellow onlookers figured it was drug related. This place had a horrible reputation. She'd never been here in her life, not even on this street, and now she knew why. Figured it's where Waylon and Bobby Ray spent their time.

Her thoughts quickly drifted to Waylon and a lump formed in her throat. They'd basically left him there to be killed, but she wasn't ready to die for him either. Not after all the shit he'd put her through, and dammit, his life choices simply sucked; nothing she could do about that. But, still, she felt bad if that's what that shot they'd heard was. She debated on running back inside, but what would that have done other than making her a witness to a murder or at least a witness to see Marcus standing over him with a gun or dragging him away or something? And, likely, Ford would never have let her go back inside anyway.

An officer walked out of the bar, and she cranked her neck to see inside. All she saw was a darkened doorway and a darker interior. Probably to mask its occupants as they were making their drug deals. She inched a bit closer to the side of the building, a few steps from the police car she'd been standing behind when she heard a loud bang. A wall on the side of the building broke open, and a man came running out like he was on fire. Dirty white T-shirt, at least it looked like it was supposed to be white, ripped up jeans and tennis shoes that looked the worse for wear. The mop of dirty brown hair flopped with each step he took, but all she could see was the back of his head because he kept looking behind him at the building. She frantically looked around for smoke, worried that a fire had started and Ford was inside. That's when she was grabbed around the waist and pulled into his smelly flabby belly.

His bad breath assaulted her nostrils, and he said close to her face, "You're mine now, Megan June. You're my way out of here alive."

Dread filled her stomach as a gun was jammed into her ribs, his beefy arm wrapped around her neck and dragged her back along the street. Screaming and yelling sounded from the onlookers, and her eyes frantically sought Ford. Just as she thought of him, he appeared from the same opening Bobby Ray had run from, and the look on his face when he saw her dragged along by Bobby Ray was scary indeed. His jaw tightened. Even from this distance, she could see the murderous look on his face.

"Back up, Montgomery. I'll kill her for sure."

To make his point, he jerked roughly on her neck, briefly

held up his gun for everyone to see and then shoved it back into her ribs causing her to wince.

Her head was slowly coming around to what had just happened and to say she wished more than anything that she was pointing the gun at Bobby Ray would be an understatement. As far as she was concerned, he could go to hell with Waylon and they'd both probably piss Satan off so damn much they'd be expelled from hell. Wouldn't that be funny?

Ford slowly took a step forward, and Bobby Ray jerked her again which halted Ford's progress. She placed both of her hands on his pasty forearm, as much to give her something to hold on to as to keep the pressure off her throat. Why hadn't she taken jujitsu classes with Jolie when she'd wanted to go? This would have been a great time to use it.

The officer who'd been standing by the car was on his radio, and the officer at the barricade had his gun trained on Bobby Ray which also meant on her by default. An officer standing next to Ford also had his gun pointed at them and who knew how many more were inside? What struck her as weird was Ford did not have his gun raised at them, his was pointing to the ground. And, at a time like this, why would stupid things like that stick out in her mind?

Ford held out his hand and slowly knelt down to lay his gun on the ground. "Bobby Ray, I've laid my gun down. Let Megan go. She has nothing to do with any of this." He took a step forward. "This is between you and me."

"Not one more step, Ford, or Megan will be going to live with your parents."

That made Ford's lip curl up in a snarl, and Bobby Ray chuckled. Her stomach turned at the taunt. How could he or anyone for that matter, be so blasé about killing someone? He wasn't a human being anymore; he was an animal.

Her stomach rolled at the stench of his breath, clothes, and this whole situation. How did she continue to get into shit like this? Closing her eyes for a moment to think without looking at the sea of horrified faces staring at her, she tried taking a cleansing breath, but the pressure on her throat made it impossible. Then she thought she could use that to her advantage.

"Bobby Ray, I can't ..." She struggled. "... breathe."

"Shut the fuck up, bitch."

"Can't." She made herself sound as pitiful as possible then let herself go limp. Her mind told her to let herself fall to the ground, a bruise or even a broken bone here and there would heal. Bobby Ray grunted as her weight became too much to handle and he dropped her like a sack of rocks.

"Megan." She heard Ford yell her name but was afraid to let him know she was okay in case Bobby Ray stood there.

Screaming sounded from the crowd then she heard fists hitting flesh, and she braved a look for herself. Men in the crowd descended on Bobby Ray, a couple of them beating the daylights out of him, the cops now jumping into the fray. Ford dropped down beside her and quickly scooped her up. "Megan!" his strained voice yelled out.

"I'm okay, Ford; go get your collar."

His hands framed her face. "Go. I'm good."

He swiftly kissed her lips then ran off toward the fighting in the street.

As she got to her feet, one of the paramedics came to her aid. "You all right?" he asked.

She smiled at him. "Shaken but fine."

"Ma'am, please come to the ambulance and let us make sure. Plus, you'll be out of the crush of bodies."

She nodded, and he assisted her to the large red vehicle.

Her knees were wobbly, and now that the fear had time to sink in, her whole body shook uncontrollably.

Another paramedic wrapped a silver heat generating blanket around her shoulders, "It's the adrenaline hitting all at once. You'll be fine in a few minutes once it dissipates," he explained.

She nodded as he handed her a bottle of water. Then he shined a light in her eyes to see that her pupils dilated properly. Once the spots left her vision, she looked over to see a very angry Ford, with a bright red welt on his jaw and his hands on Bobby Ray with a police officer walking toward one of the police cars. Bobby Ray's hands were cuffed behind his back, and once Ford roughly shoved him into the back seat of the car, the officer leaned in and cuffed Bobby Ray's ankles to the floor. Doubtful he'd be going anywhere. For good measure, three more officers stood around the car watching him to make sure he didn't pull any crap.

Ford stood talking to the officers for a few moments, then pulled his phone from his back pocket. Pushing a couple of buttons, he looked up to see her sitting at the back of the ambulance and headed her way. Even disheveled, hair mussed, shirt ripped, and reddened jaw, he was everything and more than any woman could want. Tall, broad shouldered, muscular, dark hair and eyes and that sexy low voice. Plus, he was loving and kind and good.

"Emmy, I got him." His eyes met hers. "We got him."

He smiled and pulled the phone away from his ear, and she could hear Emmy yelling and cheering. People in the background with her were cheering as well. His kissed her lips then smiled at her. "We got him," he whispered.

She nodded and returned his smile.

"Are you okay?"

"I'm fine." Her hand touched his jaw. "What about you?"

"Bastard got a punch in, but that was it. I got in a few more."

He held up his hand, and she saw the angry red knuckles, which were going to be sore tomorrow.

He finished his conversation with Emmy, and she realized two things. One, she wanted Ford Montgomery with her whole heart. And, two, she loved him, but he was still married, and that was a problem.

CHAPTER 38

Finishing his call with Emmy, who promised to call Dawson, he sat next to Megan at the back of the ambulance as one of the paramedics lay an ice pack over his knuckles and examined his jaw. Nothing was broken, but he'd be sore tomorrow. Both of them had had the day of all days. He turned to face her, the silver wrap around her shoulders catching the sunlight and lighting up her face. It was like looking at an angel, the evangelical glow surrounding her, bathing her in holy light. At least, that's what she looked like to him.

Seeing a black streak in his peripheral vision, he glanced up at an approaching black Charger and chuckled. "Rory's here to congratulate me."

Setting the ice bag to the side, he nodded to the paramedic and stood. Megan stood with him, and he took her hand, moving them toward his friend. Rory saw them walking forward and met them halfway. Embracing his old friend, they hugged, slapped each other's backs, and chuckled.

"Congratulations, Ford. I never doubted you'd get him."

"Thanks, Rory. I couldn't have done it without all of your help. Thanks for everything."

His friend turned to stare at Megan, a broad smile on his face.

"Rory, this is Megan."

"I am very, very pleased to meet you, Megan. You must be so happy this is all over." His bigger hand held out toward hers, and he saw her smile fall. Then as if she realized he was watching her, she plastered a fake smile on. "I am, yes. Thank you for all of your help."

Rory's head cocked to the side, his brows furrowing slightly before looking back at him. "So, I've spoken to the officers, and we have a prison transport on its way with four armed guards. He won't be pulling his disappearing stunt again."

"I figured as much." Worried about Megan, Ford wrapped his arm around her shoulders and pulled her close.

Rory turned to Megan. "Megan, I'm sorry to be the one to have to tell you this, but your ex-husband was mortally wounded in a shooting over on Chestnut Street. It appears it was a drug deal gone bad."

She nodded her head but said nothing for a few moments, swallowing a couple of times. "Thank you for telling me, Rory. He didn't hang out with the best of people." Her lips thinned to a straight line, her shoulders slumped, and he hoped guilt wasn't creeping in.

"That's for certain." Glancing toward the cop car and Bobby Ray, he continued, "You've got the collar, Ford. The reward will be yours. I'll need you to come to the station and sign some paperwork once I have it all in place. It has to make its rounds with South Pass PD and then over to me. I'll call you in a day or two to settle it all up."

He gently slapped his friend on the shoulder. "Sounds good, Rory, and thanks again."

"Nice meeting you, Megan. I'm sure I'll see you around."

She smiled, and Rory turned and walked away.

His stomach tightened at the somber mood that hung over them. She should be relieved. Instead she seemed apprehensive and about to cry. Turning to face her, he softly brushed his fingers over the red marks on her neck. They'd be gone in an hour or two, but when he saw Bobby Ray holding her and shoving a gun in her ribs, he'd just about lost it. If she'd been hurt, or worse, none of this would have been worth it. Not by a long shot.

"Does it hurt?"

"No," she replied. "And the shaking has almost stopped."

Pulling her chin up, so her eyes met his, he studied her. Tapping the top of her head twice, he asked, "How about up here?"

"I'm fine, Ford."

"You don't seem fine. What's going on, Meg?"

"How did he get over to Chestnut Street? And, it seems like my fault, I assumed he wouldn't fair well with Marcus, but ..."

"Hey." Her sad green eyes bored into his. "It was a shitty decision for anyone to have to make. You or him. No one wants to have to make a decision like that. But, I made that one. Me. I told you to get out. I forced you out, Meg. I can bear that on my shoulders; you don't have to."

Her eyes glittered with fresh tears. As the moisture gathered in the corners of her eyes, he swiped the fresh tears away.

"I didn't have to listen to you."

"Yes, you did. You can't honestly believe Marcus would have left you alive after you witnessed him kill Waylon."

She swallowed. Her lips parted as if she had something to say, but nothing came out. "They live a different life, Meg. They care about drugs and money. Life means squat to people like that. Do you get me?"

Her head nodded slightly since he still held her chin. She swiped her tongue over her lips. "You didn't point your gun at Bobby Ray."

His brows furrowed. "What?"

"Everyone else had their guns pointed at Bobby Ray when he had me in front of him, but you didn't."

Releasing her chin, he dragged his fingers through her hair and held her head, the silken drape over his raw knuckles a balm. "I wasn't going to risk accidentally shooting you. You can't possibly think it was because I didn't want to shoot him, 'cause God's honest truth, Meg, I'd like to go over and shoot him in that car right the fuck now for touching even a hair on your head." His fingers moved to the marks on her neck, softly petting the reddened skin. "In my anger, I was afraid I'd make a mistake."

The flood gates opened then, and her tears flowed like an opening dam. He pulled her to his chest and wrapped his arms tightly around her. She felt good, fit him perfectly.

South Pass Chief of Police, Chief Monroe, strode to them. "Prison transport is here, Ford. Unless you have something important to add regarding the events here today, you're both free to go."

Her sad eyes, still the color of fresh spring grass captured his and his body zinged to life. She had that effect on him.

"Are you ready to go?"

Her doleful lips trembled with a half-smile. "Yeah."

213

"Where am I taking you?"

Her body stiffened in his arms, and she stepped away from him. Hurt crushed her features, and he shook his head to catch up to what was happening here.

"I don't ..." Her lips trembled, but she pulled them between her teeth. Taking a deep breath, then exhaling, she continued, "I don't have anywhere to go."

CHAPTER 39

This was it. She'd been dreading it most of the day. Of everything else that was going on, she knew he'd break up with her. Not that they were together; he was still married, after all, but he'd tell her they were through. It sunk like a dagger in her heart. Hot, blazing, and damaging as if he had actually pierced her with a knife. She didn't want to cry in front of him. Through all of this, she'd been amazingly stoic and brave, but now ... now she felt like she would be reduced to a pile of ash in a split second.

"What do you mean by that?" His handsome face held concern and something she couldn't describe.

"I mean, my house is all but gone, and I don't think I can even live there anymore knowing ..."

He closed the distance between them, his masculine scent wrapping itself around her, that smoky leather smell mixed in with a bit of muskiness from his exertion earlier. Oh, how she'd miss that smell.

"Megan, honey. You have an Airbnb for tonight if you want it."

Oh. God. How humiliating. Her knees threatened to buckle.

"Or we can go home to Lynyrd Station on the Hill."

Her eyes snapped to his. Did he just say what she thought he said? "What?"

"You can't have thought after all of this that I'd just let you walk out of my life." He gently took her hands in his, kissed the knuckles on each hand then lifted her chin with his warm, strong fingers to his face—the face she wanted to look at forever. Everywhere. Sitting across from her at the table. Waking up with him each morning. Smiling at her from his desk. Hell, even scowling at her.

"Megan, honey, I've fallen in love with you. Please tell me you feel the same way."

"You love me?" She couldn't have heard that right. He loved her? It seemed too soon, and yet, it felt like she'd known him for years. Forever. He felt so right in her life, but it seemed impossible.

He laughed then. His dark eyes, framed with those impossibly thick lashes, the lines at the corners of his eyes a little more pronounced today than they had been yesterday and even this morning.

"Yes." He kissed her lips softly, his chuckles entering her mouth. His warm body pressed against hers, his hands holding her head gently but firmly to his.

"I love you too."

He picked her up and spun them around so fast she had to hold on to him tightly. No hardship there. When he stopped spinning them, he continued to hold her off the ground, but he kissed her again, then his laughing interrupted. "You thought I was breaking up with you."

"No, I didn't."

He threw his head back, and oh, it was beautiful. There

was nothing more exciting and gorgeous than smiling Ford. "Yes, you did."

"Hey, get a room," Rory yelled as he walked back to his car. The prison transport van, loaded with Bobby Ray June and four armed guards pulled out just in front of him.

Setting her on the ground, Ford gave Rory the finger and promptly got one right back. Those deep dark eyes set on her again and his equally dark brows rose into his adorably tousled coal black hair. "Where are we going?"

"Lynyrd Station on the Hill."

CHAPTER 40

Pulling up to his driveway, he let out a curse. "Well, fuck."

Emmy's truck, Dawson's truck, and his nephew Dillon's truck were in the driveway. Every damned light in the house was on, and the music pumping through his stereo system could be heard before the garage door opened.

Glancing over to see Megan's reaction, she grinned, pretty as a picture, that very first picture he'd seen of her had captured his heart, but sitting here now with her, there was no comparison. "Looks like we're having a party."

"I wanted to have a private naked party." His mood was just south of dark because that thought had been running through his mind every mile they drove to get here.

She giggled, then leaned over the console and kissed his lips. "We can do that after this party. And that one doesn't have to end for a long time."

Her nose still touching his as her lips brought his thoughts to life made his heart hammer. He grasped her head between his hands and kissed her lips, driving his tongue into her mouth. "I do like the way you think. Why don't we make out here?"

"Uncle Ford is kissing," came the innocent comment from one of his nieces.

"Grr." He looked out the side window where his niece Jessica, Dawson's youngest, stood to look at them, the door to the house stood open and his sister and brother-in-law, Scott, looking out at them from the doorway.

Megan's cheeks turned an irresistible shade of red, and she flopped back into her seat, "Oh my God."

Chuckling, he opened his door, bending down to scoop Jessica up in his arms as she dove at him. Carrying her around to the passenger side of the truck, he opened the door and held his hand out to help Megan step down.

"I saw you kissing Uncle Ford. I'm Jessica."

"Hi Jessica, I'm Megan. How old are you?"

"I'm eight. How old are you?"

"Never mind, Jess." He chuckled again and took Megan's hand in his, giving her a squeeze. Emmy stepped from the doorway and hugged him with Jessica in his arm then gave Megan a good long squeeze. As they entered the house to the noise and commotion, they were enveloped by his family as introductions and drinks were passed around. This felt pretty damned awesome.

As he looked around the house, the smiles on his family made this feel so much better. They'd all been through so much. Megan too. Now it felt like they all had good things happening to them.

He leaned against his desk, a glass of bourbon in his hand watching Megan chat with the kids and with Dawson's wife, Sylvia. Her smile brightened the whole room. The kids gravitated to her and more than ever he wished Falcon were here to meet her. He'd never had much of a mother figure in his life. He'd love Megan. She was the perfect blend of strength and affection.

"You love her?" Emmy leaned on the desk next to him, their bodies side by side staring out at their family.

"Yep."

"You tell her?"

"Yep."

"Now what?"

He looked down into his sister's deep brown eyes, so much like his own. "I have to get divorced, Emmy. I tried making a deal with Stephano today. A touch on the illegal side at that, but I need to move on, and I want to move on with Megan. Even if it means I have to leave here."

Emmy stared across the room at the gathering and joviality of their loved ones, her head nodding. "I hope that doesn't happen, and I'll help in any way I can."

Taking a swig from his drink, he kissed his sister on the top of her head and pulled her forward into the fray.

———

M egan giggled. "I think my ears are ringing from all of the noise." She set her wineglass in the dishwasher and turned to face him as he closed and locked the door. He walked to his computer to set the security system, and when he looked up, Megan stood next to the kitchen counter naked as the day she was born, but much, much sexier. He was positive of that. He could feel the smile crawl across his face. It was both a pleasant surprise and raw, sexual excitement.

"Now that is a sight I will never tire of."

As she walked toward him, her full breasts mesmerized him with their gentle sway. When he was able to pull his eyes away from the hypnotic dance of her breasts, they dropped to the narrow patch of auburn curls. He licked his lips, remembering her taste.

Stopping in front of him, her hands immediately went to his T-shirt and lifted it up over his body. He took over when her reach became too short, but he was happy for it because her hands roamed his body, then her tongue dipped into each valley between his abdominal muscles, and his cock swelled painfully thick. She swirled her tongue around his navel as her fingers worked the button on his jeans. The zipper lowered, and his cock surged forward as if a divining rod seeking gold or oil. He wasn't disappointed when she dropped to her knees before him, her pink tongue leaving a wet path on her lips. His eyes were locked on the sight before him, her wild auburn head dipped to lower his jeans to his feet, helping him step from each leg in turn. As her hands gripped his boxer briefs, he felt the moisture at the tip of his eager cock dampen them. She hummed her appreciation, and he thought his knees would buckle, the only thing keeping them locked was the need of her mouth on his cock.

He didn't have to wait long. Her gentle fingers pulled his length to her waiting mouth. She swiped the thick broad head of his cock along the seam of her lips and hummed. Tilting her head up just enough for their eyes to meet, his breath held. Her sweet lips pursed to kiss the throbbing member in her hands just before she lowered her head and took him into her hot, wet mouth.

Spellbound at the sight of Megan on her knees sucking his cock, he willed himself to breathe once again. The warmth of her tongue sliding along the underside of his cock made his heart race double time. Her other hand cupped his balls and gave them a gentle squeeze, and his

221

cock twitched. She worked him then, up and down on his shaft, the sight of it something he wanted to commit to memory forever, and the feel of it something he'd never be able to describe. His legs shook with the effort to control his orgasm, which was coming at blinding speed. The tightness at the base of his spine building his cock so hot and hard he feared it would split open.

He panted, unable to speak the words he needed to say. "Megan."

He slid his hand into the soft curls on the top of her head, and the erotic feel of her head bobbing as she took him into her warmth increased the excitement of this moment. "I'm going to ..."

Her head worked faster, she swallowed, and her throat closed around his cock as she took him all the way in. That was the end of it. It felt like time stood still as he spilled himself inside her mouth. Her rapid swallowing of all he had to offer was without a doubt a moment he'd never forget.

A droplet of sweat trickled down the middle of his back as she hummed and continued licking him as his cock softened. She palmed his balls, now dropping into her waiting hand and with a final kiss on his softened penis, her eyes turned up to his, and a soft smile grew on her face.

"I've never done that before." The pink of her tongue appeared at the corner of her mouth, licking away an errant smear, but his mind struggled to focus. She was damned near dangerous to him if she could make his mind blank like that.

His brows raised as her words registered. "No?" Before he actually dropped to the floor, he knelt with her, the burning wood in the fire place still offering them warmth, and the crackling now reaching his ears after the deafening thrum of his blood coursing through them.

Wrapping an arm around her back, he lay her down on the cream colored deep pile rug he had scoffed at when Emmy brought it here. Now though, he'd love it always from this memory alone. "For a beginner, you're simply fantastic." Kissing her lips, his taste still on her breath, sent signals to his cock and the slow re-thickening tensed his muscles.

He kissed his way down her body, amazed as the goose-flesh formed on her creamy skin. Feeling the patch of hair on his lips, he kissed then blew on her, loving the squirm it elicited from her responsive body. Sliding back to drink in the sight of her, laying here in front of the fire, in his home, ready and welcoming him into her body and he'd do just that. Itching to touch her, sample her wetness, he slid a finger along her seam, thrilled to see the moisture gather. Running that moisture up and over her clit, he divided his attention between watching her pussy dance and her face as the pleasure washed over her. Testing her body to see what she wanted and needed, he added pressure to her clit as his swirling finger closed in closer to the now swelling bud. Her hips flexed and rose, and he knew now where he'd focus his attention first. Lowering his mouth around her pink pussy, he sucked her clit into his mouth and was welcomed with a low erotic moan.

Alternating between sucking her in and rolling his tongue over her, his pleasure mounted as hers was coming to her release. Her fingers dug roughly into his hair, fisting his head between her hands, the sting of pain in his scalp further hardening his cock. One final hard suck on her and she cried out her orgasm, as he lapped at her sweet juices, his new favorite taste. As her thighs stopped shaking, he climbed over her body and thrust himself into her, eager to spill himself just one more time tonight in her body.

Her legs lifted and wrapped around his ass, her heels digging in, pushing him in farther. This was not a long sweet mating, this was fierce full-on desire and a claiming of sorts. In some way, they'd both ways just claimed each other, and he felt wild and free and so very eager to stake his claim once again.

She cried out as her orgasm hit, and his thrusts increased in speed and intensity, his seed spilling into her soon after.

CHAPTER 41

S he woke to birds singing and the sun streaming in
through the open curtains. Ford's heavy muscled arm
wrapped tightly around her waist, her back to his front, not
an ounce of space between them.

This is how she'd woken every morning for the past
three months since their ridiculous journey back to South
Pass and all that had happened there. They'd settled into
life here, Ford deciding once and for all he was retiring from
bounty hunting, but the calls kept coming in. She wanted
him to do what he wanted and not worry about her. She'd
be here, keeping house, tending the garden he'd built her on
the side of the house where she could see the back garage,
the house, and the view, while she nurtured her newly
sprouting snap peas, carrots, and lettuce.

But, today, they were hosting a picnic here at the house
to celebrate. Emmy had sped into action after Bobby Ray
was captured again and got a very agreeable judge to push
through his conviction. They'd already had a jury selected
from before, and the video of him escaping and the evidence

of him setting the fire that killed the Montgomerys was more than enough to put him away for the rest of his life.

The Wicked Witch theme song sounded on Ford's phone, and he groaned. "She's got to go," he mumbled into her neck before rolling over and snatching his phone off the nightstand.

She agreed, but there'd been no movement on that front. She was with Ford, she'd be here for him, but she wanted him to be hers, lock, stock, and barrel. Without him chained to another woman, even if it was on paper only.

"What?" He snapped into the phone.

Staring at the ceiling, she mused over whether she'd give him privacy to talk to her or stay and listen. Usually, when she pulled away, he grabbed her and pulled her closer. But, she had things to do to get ready. She was making apple pies today and a lot of them. The Montgomery family ate them as if they'd be their last.

Ford sat bolt upright which halted her leaving. Sitting alongside him, she willed her heart to slow its rapid beating. Hopefully, nothing had happened to Falcon. She'd just spoken to him on the phone last night. The three of them now had weekly Skype calls, and she enjoyed getting to know him a bit better. He'd be home in four months.

"You better not be shitting me, Tamra. I've had enough."

His eyes sought hers, his brows raised high into his hairline. "Okay."

Ending the call, he tossed it to the foot of the bed and claimed her lips, his kiss urgent and gentle at the same time. Not sure how to feel about him getting hot and bothered after speaking with his wife on the phone, she tried enjoying his mouth against hers, but it wasn't working this morning.

He pulled back and stared into her eyes, his still the color of ebony. "I'm getting a divorce."

The slow smile that spread his kiss swollen lips was mesmerizing. "What?"

He kissed her again, then leaned back, his hand resting just below her breasts, close to her heart. "Stephano threatened to cut her off if she didn't sign the papers. He's had enough too. That was the trick apparently. She wants a fast divorce, so she and Stephano can marry. She signed the papers last night, and Stephano has already dropped them off at her lawyer's office."

Her hands framed his handsome face, his coal black hair striped with silver threads still sleep mussed but so damned handsome. Tears filled her eyes and his visage blurred. "Really? I mean, really?"

His lips sought hers gently, and she eagerly kissed him back. Her body already eager to join with his. "Yes. Really." As he rose over her, settling between her legs, she let the tears spill. Life was finally going to be good to them both. She just had one more secret to share with him.

CHAPTER 42

Here they are, all signed. You simply have to wait sixty days, per the state of Indiana, and the court will finalize your divorce." Emmy beamed as she delivered the news and the signed papers. "I took the liberty of walking down the hall to Jason's office to make sure he'd gotten a copy. He had a courier run to Tamra's lawyer's office to pick them up."

Hugging his sister, he whispered in her ear, "Thank you, Em."

Her arms squeezed his waist. She'd always had his back, even as kids, but she'd gone above and beyond as they'd grown to adulthood. He regretted saddling this family with Tamra. He didn't regret Falcon, but he regretted everything else they'd all been through because of him and his decisions.

She pulled back and stared him in the eye. "You're welcome. You can thank me by making that beautiful woman over there your wife. She's perfect."

"You have no idea." He chuckled and was pleased to see

how fond his sister was of Megan. They watched as Megan carried two more pies from the house and out to the picnic tables they'd set up to hold the whole family, all except Falcon, who they'd join in on a group call in an hour. His family clapped as she set the pies down and she laughed and jumped back when they descended on them like locusts. "Don't you ever feed your family?" he teased.

"That's not all mine. Dawson and the kids are jumping in there, too."

"She makes pies like Mom, have you noticed?"

"I have." She chuckled then her voice softened. "I see she's trying her hand at painting like mom too. I saw the picture on the barn boards in the kitchen."

Swallowing the lump in his throat and blinking to keep the tears in check, all he could say was, "Yeah."

Dillon's truck finally appeared in the driveway. He'd had soccer practice today and pulled in just in time for dessert.

"Okay, we're all here, I have an announcement to make," he said to Emmy.

Walking to Megan, she turned and smiled, her face a beacon to his ship. The sun glinted off her auburn mane of wild curls, her green eyes rivaled the grass on the lawn. She wore wild colored leggings of black with bright blues, greens and yellow flowers covering them. She'd been wearing the leggings lately, telling him they felt like she was encased in soft butter. The bright blue, loose fitting T-shirt she wore tied in a cute little knot on the side by her hip.

He bent and kissed her lips, then cleared his throat and looked at his family sitting at the two picnic tables pulled together and covered in red and white checked cloths.

"I'd like to say something." They stopped their ravenous eating, a few grumbling in the process, but looked at him as he stared back. "You all have been with me through thick and thin, and I'd like to thank you so much for being here for me. I only hope to be as good to you as you've been to me. Especially you, Emmy; you've been my rock."

Emmy raised her glass to him and winked. "You've been there for us too, Ford. You have no idea how much."

Swallowing the dry lump that appeared, he cleared his throat. "Anyway, I'm glad you're all here because I've waited what feels like a lifetime to say this."

He turned to Megan and was rewarded with a smile that took his breath away. He dropped to one knee and heard several gasps, then silence. Pulling a small box from his pocket, he lifted the lid and turned it toward her. "Megan, will you marry me?"

He saw the tears fill her eyes and escape down her cheeks as she stared at the box. Her shaking fingers lifted the chain with the diamond encrusted necklace from it. The diamonds glittered in the sunlight, raining sparkles on her face and hair, across her chest and arms. Laying on the cross was the diamond ring he'd bought for her.

"Where did you get this?"

"Waylon stole it. I found it in the shack, but he'd pried most of the diamonds from it, probably to sell. I took it to a jeweler and had it repaired and the ring made to match it."

Swallowing profusely, she lay the cross in her hand and fingered the ring. The full two carat diamond in the center was held in place by the matching filigree on the cross, diamonds set into the band matching her prized possession.

"Oh. My. God." She whispered it, but they all heard. His heart pounded as he watched the emotions in her dazzling face. Clasping the cross and the ring tightly in her fist, she held them to her heart, a sob escaping as she tried holding it in. Her watery eyes captured his and held. Softly, she said, "Yes." She pulled him up with her free hand and wrapped both arms around his neck, squeezing her body to his. "Yes, we will marry you."

He pulled back, his brows furrowed, seeking clarification. Her bright eyes danced back and forth as she stared into his eyes. "I'm pregnant. We're pregnant."

He whooped loud into the air, their audience cheered as they were enveloped in the many arms of his loving family. Hugs and kisses aplenty.

———

E njoying their after-breakfast routine of sitting at the kitchen table with their laptops, he looked up from the email he read from his battle brother, Lincoln.

"Lincoln wants to join forces with me and open an agency. We'll employ bounty hunters and spread out all over the country finding the Bobby Rays of the world. What do you think of that?"

Her green eyes darted to his, a smile spreading across her flushed cheeks as excitement rose in her body. She laughed, and the sight was one to behold. "That's perfect, Ford. Oh my God, that is just perfect. You said you wanted to retire, but instead, you can still be in the bounty hunting game but from the safer vantage point of the business side of things. That's brilliant."

She jumped up from her chair and came around the table. He pulled her down on his lap, her belly just beginning to round with their child, to read the email.

"Who's Dodge?"

"Another of our battle brothers. We used to laugh at the

three of us, each named after cars, so we were nicknamed the Hot Rods."

Twisting slightly, she looked into his eyes. "Hot Rod Bounty Hunters. I love it."

He chuckled. "We'll work on the name. But first, we have a wedding to plan and a baby to grow."

CHAPTER 43

I t was probably silly, but she didn't want to take any chances. The bride and groom weren't supposed to see each other the day of the wedding until the groom saw the bride walking down the aisle. Ford refused to stay down at the cabin he lived in on Emmy's property because, dammit, he didn't want to sleep anywhere but where she and the baby slept, but she worried about that goofy old wives' tale. So, Ford slept in the spare room—the room she first stayed in—insisting she sleep in their room.

So, here she was in their bedroom, lying in their super comfy bed, lovingly rubbing her burgeoning belly and sending love thoughts to their baby, waiting for Ford to get out of the house. Dawson was coming to pick him up and take him down to the church to get ready, then Emmy would be here to pick her up. Ford's nephew, Dillon, had taken his truck home last night so they could decorate it. Neither she nor Ford were allowed to see it until they exited the church. She was almost a bit scared about that.

Her phone played "Everything I Do" by Bryan Adams and the instant smile that appeared on her face and the giggle that sounded was that of a lovesick schoolgirl, but she didn't care.

"Good morning."

She heard his deep intake of breath. "It isn't bad luck to talk on the phone before the wedding, is it?"

She giggled again. "No, it isn't bad luck to talk on the phone. Are you about ready to leave?"

"Soon. Dawson is on his way, and since I can't come in and kiss you and steal a bit of lovin', I at least wanted to say good morning."

"You never have to steal lovin', Ford; it's here for you always." She closed her eyes and laid back. "Just not this morning." She giggled as he groaned. "But tonight, now that's a whole new thing. Tonight, you'll make love to your wife."

"First time in my life that sounds perfect. I can't wait."

She sat up to lean back against the headboard. "Did you sleep well last night?"

"No."

A smile spread across her face. "Ah, you missed my big ole belly pushing into your back."

"Honey, I missed all of you. Every damned inch. But I'm going to make up for it later."

"Good."

Beeping sounded from the computer in the living room. "Daws is here. I'll see you in about two hours, darlin'. Stay safe while we're apart. Love you."

"I love you, too, Ford."

The call ended, and she listened for the door to open and close. Peering out the bedroom window to the side, she watched as Dawson drove him away down the driveway. Now it was time to get her day rolling.

Stepping into the bathroom to get the shower warming,

she looked at herself in the mirror. Her face had filled out just like her belly, and now her ankles were starting to swell too. She wasn't quite six months pregnant, and she'd gained around eight pounds, which her doctor told her was normal, but it felt like so much more. She waited until the last minute to buy her wedding dress because she didn't know how much she'd gain by their wedding day.

Gathering her new undergarments, pantyhose, and garter, she stepped back into the bathroom. Letting the water spray over her, she closed her eyes enjoying the solitude, warm water, and the loving the anticipation of what's to come. Her phone rang and broke the moment, but she let it go to voicemail and finished her shower.

As she stepped out of the shower, her phone rang again; someone was insistent. Wrapping a big, green, fluffy towel around her body, she stepped into the bedroom to see who was so persistent in calling her. Looking at the readout on her phone, she saw Delaney had called three times. Now what?

Swiping the screen and tapping her sister's number, she sat on the edge of the bed while she waited for her sister to pick up.

"It's about time. I've left several messages."

"I know; I was in the shower. What's up?"

"Cord probably isn't going to make it to the wedding. They had an issue on the oil rig, and he was held back. I'm really sorry, Meg."

"Oh, crap. I haven't seen him in more than eight months; I was so hoping he'd be here. Who's going to give me away now?"

"I'll give you away, happily."

"You don't have to sound so damned happy about it."

"I'm not really happy about it, Megan. The three of us

haven't been in the same town since Grandma died. And you're the first one to have a baby, so I'm really excited to see you fat."

"Gawd, Delaney, what the hell is wrong with you?"

Her sister scoffed. "Well, if you want me to give you away, I'll do it. Otherwise, I'll just sit in the congregation since Ford's family is part of the ceremony, and I'm not."

Her stomach twisted. This is not how she wanted this morning to start. Delaney's animosity toward her hadn't let up at all. She'd hoped the fact that they'd had a couple of phone calls over the past couple of months things had settled, but apparently, they hadn't.

"I'll let you know. I've gotta get ready to head to the church. I'll see you later, Dee."

Her sister abruptly ended the call, more than likely a little bit irritated that she was getting married—for the second time—and Delaney still hadn't found anyone to marry her. But, that was because of her choices.

Tossing her phone on the bed, she scraped her hands through her wet hair. She stood and glanced out the window at the picturesque view she had every day and tried to forget Delaney's sour attitude and remember what today was all about. Ford.

Chimes rang on the computer, and she glanced out the window to see Emmy flying up the driveway. "Holy cats, what on earth is going on?"

Quickly pulling on her undergarments and pantyhose, she slipped into a pair of leggings and a loose-fitting top, still trying to towel her hair dry as she made her way to the door. They had a new understanding now; Emmy didn't just barge in any more. Not after she walked in on her and Ford making love on the sofa. Good lord, that was mortifying. She got to the door about the same time as

Emmy, and her future sister-in-law rushed in, dang near out of breath.

"Emmy, what's up?"

"Oh, God, I thought I'd be late. Dillon hurt himself at soccer this morning, and I had to rush him to the hospital. He's fine, just three stitches in his leg from a cleat, but I thought I was going to be late." Emmy stood by the kitchen counter, her ever-present lime green water bottle in her hand. "We need to get going, girl; do you have all of your stuff pulled together?"

"I was just ..."

Brushing past her, Emmy took over. "Here, I'll get your dress; you toss everything else into a bag, and we'll take off. I have to pick Raye Ann up at the house on the way through, then I have to run a quick errand while you're having your hair done."

Emmy strutted to the closet, pulled her dress from inside and held it up. "I can't wait for Ford to see you in this."

The strapless, light floral gown, which was shorter in the front, just showing off her ankles and cute strappy shoes, was the perfect dress for her. The sweetheart neckline would allow her grandmother's cross necklace as her something old, her engagement ring as her something new, and Emmy loaned her a lace handkerchief which had been her mother's, which meant so much to her and to Ford. The only thing missing was the blue.

"I hope he likes it. We both know he's all about green now, so that's one plus."

Emmy laughed, and she was amazed at how much better it made her feel. "Honey, he'd love you in a gunny sack. The man is positively head over heels for you."

Turning to her, she took the three steps that separated

them. Placing a hand on her shoulder, Emmy said, "We're all so happy he found you. Mom and Dad would be so thrilled to see him marry you."

Megan's eyes welled with tears and a lump formed in her throat. "I hope so," she managed and then was afraid to say more. Taking a deep breath, she changed the subject. "My brother, Cord, can't make it today. The rig he's on had some issues, and he's stuck there for a bit. I don't have anyone to give me away."

"Oh, damn. I'm sorry, Meg. I'll bet Dillon would be happy to walk you down the aisle."

"He has stitches in his leg; I'm not going to ask him to do that."

"Well, let me worry about that. I'll take care of it. Now, are you ready? We have to get going."

CHAPTER 44

Dawson's house was always busy. Four kids, a dog, and Dawson and Sylvia made for much more activity than Ford was used to, and to be honest, he was already on high nerves with today's excitement in the air. So sitting here now, waiting while Dawson and Sylvia ran around getting the kids ready, he was about to jump out of his own skin. He wanted to be married already, and he wanted to be holding his wife, their child nestled between the two of them.

A loud crash sounded from the back of the house, and Mark, the youngest at eight years old, yelled. The dog, a yellow lab, gentle as can be, but still puppy-ish, began barking, and Sylvia sounded exasperated when she sternly said, "Mark, what on earth are you doing throwing a ball in the house? Put it down and get dressed. Now."

David, the oldest at fourteen, sat at the kitchen table across from him and shook his head. "Mark is going to end up killing my parents. He's always into shit."

Staring at his nephew, sandy brown hair like his dad, blue eyes like his mom, Ford wrestled with correcting his swearing or letting it go. He decided to let it go. Taking a deep breath, he told David, "I'm going to walk on down to the church. Tell your dad, will you? I'm too antsy to sit here, and they've got their hands full."

"Yeah. Want company?"

David looked so hopeful to be able to get out of the house with him that he didn't have the heart to say no. "It's at least a mile walk; you up for that?"

"Yeah. That's not a problem."

Nodding and standing, he replied, "Okay. Go tell your parents, and let's get rolling."

Ford's phone rang, and he pulled it from his pocket, dread weighing heavy in his gut when he saw Rory's picture. "This better not be bad news."

"Good morning to you too. Are you planning on running before the wedding or are you going to make an honest woman of Megan?"

"What do you think?"

His friend laughed. "Just thought I'd ask. Where are you?"

He glanced down the hall as David came toward him. "I'm at Dawson's, but David and I are going to start walking down to the church. It's a madhouse here."

"Let me swing by and pick you up. I got ready early, and I'm sitting here now not sure what to do with myself. David will enjoy a ride in the Charger."

"That he will. Can you get here in less than five?"

"Start your timer."

Ending the call, he motioned with his head toward the door. David headed out first. Reaching into Dawson's truck, he grabbed his suit, dress shoes, and toiletry bag. Walking to the end of the driveway, he could hear Rory's engine gunning down the road, and he had to chuckle. You'd think he was a damned teenager, not a grown-ass man.

Pulling to a stop, his smile as wide as his whole face, he chuckled, "Less than five, right?"

"Less than five."

Holding the passenger door for David as he climbed in back, Ford folded himself into the front seat, then called back to David, "Buckle up." And he did the same.

Rory eased from the curb and made it halfway down the road Dawson lived on. Looking in the mirror at David, he said, "You want to see what this baby can do?"

"God, yes. Punch it."

Before he could get a word out, Rory had punched the gas and Ford was thrown back against the seat. He had to admit, it was fun. Nearing the intersection, Rory eased off the gas, still chuckling, his smile wide.

From the back seat, David exclaimed, "That was so cool!"

"Right?" Rory's pride evident in his eyes.

A phone rang, and Rory punched a button on the dash. "Richards."

"Detective, we have an issue. A body was found out along the road on Valley Drive. Blonde woman in her forties. Possible overdose."

Ford glanced at Rory, who stared back at him and immediately pulled over to the side of the road. He softly said, "That's where Tamra lives."

Pinching his lips together, Ford only nodded, the rolling of his stomach making him nauseous.

"I'll be right there." Rory ended the call but never looked away from him.

"I'll go with you."

"Ford, not today. You don't need this, and if it's her, you don't want to see her."

"Do you mean Aunt Tamra?"

Remembering David in the backseat, Ford twisted to look at his nephew. "We don't know yet, David, but we're going to have to take you home."

"No. Let me come. I'm going to be a cop myself one day. I want to see what you all do."

"I'm not a cop and Rory is a detective, so it's a little different. Plus, your mom will kick my ass if you have nightmares."

"I won't, I swear."

Rory twisted and looked David in the eyes. "You can't get out of the car. You have to stay here. Got it?"

David nodded. Rory caught Ford's eyes and raised his brows. "Let's go, Rory."

Pulling to the side of the road, about a quarter of a mile away from the activity, Rory killed the engine of his car, pocketed the keys, and stepped out. Sticking his head back in, he stared hard at David. "Not one step out of this car."

"I won't."

Rory caught his eyes and nodded. Making their way to the tarp-covered body lying in the road, his stomach tangled with his toast and hard-boiled egg. The smell of death lingered in the air, and he had to steal himself for what he was about to see. If it was Tamra, he had to admit he knew it would happen one day. She'd been trying to kill herself for years. But, to die alongside a country road, alone, what the hell kind of person deserved that? Falcon would be beside himself, and above all else, today on his wedding day, he didn't want this anniversary to be what everyone thought of each year. Selfish, probably, but Megan sure as hell didn't deserve this.

Covering his nose and mouth with his hand, so the stench didn't tip his guts over, he approached slowly, Rory taking the lead. He recognized the cops present, nodding to each of them, handshaking not allowed right now since they were all wearing blue rubber gloves. Rory stepped to the body, and one of the cops lifted the tarp to show him the woman. Squatting down to get a closer look, Rory glanced back at him and shook his head.

Letting out a long breath, his relief a real thing, he hesitated, not sure if he wanted to know who she was and what she was doing here or not. Plus, as he glanced at his phone for the time, he only had an hour and a half before he was getting married, and he'd need to get cleaned up and dressed. He took a couple steps back and leaned against one of the police cars watching his friend work. He was a good detective and a damned good man. Hopefully, he'd find a woman one of these days. He'd been married at one time, but his wife was killed in a car accident going on seven years ago now.

Rory stood and walked toward him. "Let's go; we've got a wedding to get to."

His jaw was tight, his eyes troubled. "Who is it, Rory?"

"It's that little gal that works at the grocery store in town. She's in her forties, Ford. That shit just pisses me off. So fucking many drugs on the streets; it's hard enough keeping the kids off that shit, let alone the adults."

CHAPTER 45

Arriving at the church, Emmy helped Megan carry her dress in through the back door while she carried her toiletry bag and her shoes. It was a splurge—these shoes. But the instant she saw them, her eyes glazed over. Cute, cream-colored strappy sandals with crystals across the three crisscross straps. She'd never in her life had a pair of classy shoes like this, and she so wanted them. She'd dipped into her savings for them, and she wanted Ford to think she was the most beautiful bride he'd ever seen, and if she were honest, since she knew Tamra at one time was beautiful, she wanted to erase his memory of her walking down the aisle and replace it with her. Totally selfish and a bit insecure, but she couldn't help that. Probably hormones. Probably.

They entered a back room, and Emmy hung their dresses on the clothing rod against the wall. Their attendants were few today. Emmy was her bridesmaid; her best friend, Jolie, her matron of honor. Rory was Ford's best man, and Dawson was the groomsman. Cord was supposed to give her away, but that wasn't going to happen. And hopefully, Delaney wouldn't be too much of a pill today.

Jolie entered, her dress and bags in hand and the two women hugged and giggled.

"I am so damned happy for you, Meg. Oh, I'm so excited for today."

Laughing, she stood back, still clasping her friend's hands. "Me too. Can you believe it, Jolie, I'm finally going to be a mom *and* a wife? All my dreams coming true."

"I say it's about time."

"Where's Derek?"

"He dropped me off. He's taking the kids and the sitter to the hotel, and then he'll be right back."

She glanced at Emmy, then back to Jolie. "Do you think he'll give me away? Cord can't make it."

"Oh, honey, I'm so sorry, but I bet he'd be happy to give you away. As soon as he gets here, I'll go and talk to him."

***

Standing at the back of the church, her stomach in knots because she was excited and nervous and she couldn't find Derek, Megan lay her hand over her stomach as she waited for the organist to begin playing the wedding march.

"Well, don't you look like the most beautiful bride ever?"

She whipped around at the sound of her brother's deep voice, and tears sprang to her eyes as he scooped her up and hugged her to him. Oh, he gave the best hugs ever—besides Ford, that is.

"I thought you couldn't make it," she whispered in his ear as he hung on to her.

"I busted ass and got myself on a private plane—paid for by my boss after he heard I'd be missing my baby sister's wedding, to get here in time. I didn't want to call in case I couldn't make it."

She squeezed him tighter, her arms around his big broad shoulders. Her handsome brother was here in the flesh. His golden blond hair, a bit long on top and cut short on the sides accented those green eyes which mirrored her own. When he set her down, her shaking hands swiped under her eyes, and Emmy came forward with a tissue, trying to clean her smeared makeup as Jolie gave Cord a hug. Then she slapped him hard on the arm. "That's for making this little bride sad this morning."

"Ouch. Christ. Sorry."

She slapped him again. "You're standing in a church. Don't take the Lord's name in vain."

"Oh. Shit. Sorry." She raised her hand again, but Derek halted her. "Don't beat him up."

Shaking hands, the two men greeted each other. Derek kissed his wife, then said, "I don't think I'm needed here any longer, so I'm going to go find a seat."

He opened the door, and the organ music grew in volume. Emmy dabbed a bit more, then smiled. "I'm up first. See you up front."

She hustled to the door. Dillon and David, who had ushered, despite Dillion's fresh stitches, opened the doors and stood just inside.

Jolie winked at her, then stepped up to the door and disappeared down the aisle. Cord held out his arm to her, and she slipped her hand through the crook, grateful for his strength and his presence. "Was Delaney a bitch this morning?"

That put a smile on her face. "Yes."

"Figured. Grandma's necklace looks perfect on you."

She blinked furiously to keep the tears from sliding from her eyes.

The bridal march began playing, and the congregation stood. Her heart hammered in her chest as the sea of faces watched her walk toward her soon-to-be husband. And she almost let herself become so nervous she thought she'd throw up, but then she looked at Ford and the love in his eyes for her made her feel as if she were walking on a cloud.

His smile was a sight to behold, and he looked so sexy in his suit, the same light bluish green as her dress. The white rose pinned to his lapel looked perfect on him. His jet-black hair was combed neatly to the side, a lock falling onto his forehead, and she itched to touch it. Those obsidian eyes, shiny and framed in those sexy lashes, were what her dreams were made of. She hoped their baby looked like him.

Cord reached forward and shook Ford's hand, and whispered, "I'm happy to meet you, Ford; you're a lucky man."

"Happy to meet you, Cord, and please know that I know that with my whole heart."

Cord nodded and bent down to kiss her cheek. "I love you, Meg; congratulations, hon," he whispered.

"Thank you, Cord. I love you too."

He stepped away from her and stood next to Delaney, but she only had eyes for Ford. The minister stepped forward and cleared his throat.

"This is a special day for Megan and Ford, but it's also a special day for the whole Montgomery family." Pressing the Bible in his hands to his chest, he continued, "Many of you know that like his father before him, Falcon Montgomery, is serving in the United States Army, currently in Afghanistan. But, I'm proud to say Falcon wanted to be here today and has moved heaven and earth to get here to watch his father take a bride." Holding his hand up toward the back of the church the doors opened, and there stood a handsome man, one she'd never met but would know anywhere, in a crisp dress uniform striding purposely toward them.

Ford's deep intake of breath could be heard throughout the quiet church. He stepped down from the altar meeting his son halfway, and when they embraced, not a dry eye could be found in the house. Through her watery gaze, she gingerly stepped from the altar and joined her man and her soon-to-be stepson, and before Ford could introduce them in person, Falcon swooped down and picked her up, holding her to him. She could feel his heartbeat, his excitement; she could feel his shaking hands, and her heart went out to him.

When he set her down, Ford clapped him on the shoulder, "Come and stand with us while we say our vows, son."

Falcon's dark eyes sought hers. "Are you sure?"

She smiled. "Absolutely, Falcon. Please join us."

He nodded and swallowed, apparently overcome with emotion. He held his hand out to them to proceed before him, and they made their way back to the altar to become man and wife—their entire family there to witness it.

***

Dancing to their wedding song at the reception, he whispered in her ear, "So, let's talk about this dress."

Pulling back to look into his eyes, her brows furrowed, "What about it?"

He chuckled and pulled her into his chest once more. "You are without a doubt the most beautiful bride ever."

As he spun her around the dance floor, she couldn't help but laugh. Mission accomplished.

***

Lincoln Winters is joining forces with Ford. Grab your

copy of Finding His Mark to see how Lynyrd Station Protectors brings an Italian cartel to heel. Finding His Mark.

Get PJ's newsletter for updates on new releases, sales, fun snippets and so much more.

ALSO BY PJ FIALA

You can find all of my books at https://pjfiala.com/books

Romantic Suspense

Rolling Thunder Series

Moving to Love, Book 1

Moving to Hope, Book 2

Moving to Forever, Book 3

Moving to Desire, Book 4

Moving to You, Book 5

Moving On, Book 6

Rolling Thunder Boxset 1, Books 1-3

Rolling Thunder Boxset 2, Books 4-6

Military Romantic Suspense

Second Chances Series

Designing Samantha's Love, Book 1

Securing Kiera's Love, Book 2

Bluegrass Security Series

Heart Thief, Book One

Finish Line, Book Two

Lethal Love, Book Three

Wrenched Fate, Book Four

Lynyrd Station Protectors - Security

Finding His Fire Book One

Finding His Mark Book Two

Finding His Jewel Book Three

Finding His Match Book Four

Lynyrd Station Protectors - GHOST

Defending Keirnan, GHOST Book One

Defending Sophie, GHOST Book Two

Defending Roxanne, GHOST Book Three

Defending Yvette, GHOST Book Four

Defending Bridget, GHOST Book Five

Defending Isabella, GHOST Book Six

GHOST Box Set One (Books 1-3)

GHOST Box Set Two (Books 4-6)

Lynyrd Station Protectors - RAPTOR

RAPTOR Rising - Prequel

Saving Shelby, RAPTOR Book One

Holding Hadleigh, RAPTOR Book Two

Craving Charlesia, RAPTOR Book Three

Promising Piper, RAPTOR Book Four

Missing Mia, RAPTOR Book Five

Believing Becca, RAPTOR Book Six

Keeping Kori, RAPTOR Book Seven

Healing Hope, RAPTOR Book Eight

Engaging Emersyn, RAPTOR Book Nine

RAPTOR Box Set 1

RAPTOR Box Set 2

RAPTOR Box Set 3

GHOST Legacy (Next generation)

Finding Lara, Book One

Saving Elena, Book Two

Rescuing Kenna, Book Three

Protecting Everleigh, Book Four

Guarding Adelaide, Book Five

Shielding Maya, Book Six

DEAR READER

Thank you so much for reading Finding His Fire. Did you know that when you rate a book with only stars and no text the author does not see it? It also doesn't help us with vendor ratings either. But, by simply writing five words or more, this greatly helps us out so we can apply for promotions to further market our books. Would you please consider a few words along with your star rating? I thank you in advance and hope to see you on the internet.

Review Finding His Fire - https://geni.us/FindingHisFire

MEET PJ

I was born in a suburb of St. Louis, Missouri named Bridgeton. During my time in Missouri, I explored the Ozarks, swam in the Mississippi River, and played kickball and endless games of hide-and-seek with the neighborhood kids. The summers spent in Kentucky with my grandmother, Ruth, are the fondest childhood memories for me.

At the age of thirteen, my family moved to Wisconsin to learn to farm. Yes, learn to farm! That was interesting. Taking city kids and throwing them on a farm with twenty-eight cows purchased from the Humane Society because they had been abused was a learning experience. I learned to milk cows, the ins and outs of breeding and feeding schedules, the never-ending haying in the summer and trying to stay warm in the winter. Our first winter in Wisconsin, one storm brought 36 inches of snow, and we were snowed in for three days! Needless to say, I didn't love Wisconsin.

I'm now married with four children and four grandchildren. I have learned to love Wisconsin, though I still hate snow. My husband and I travel around by motorcycle seeing new sites and meeting new people. It never ceases to amaze me how many people are interested in where we're going and what we've seen along the way. At every gas station, restaurant, and hotel, people come up to us and ask us about what we're doing, as well as offer advice on which roads in the area are better than others.

I come from a family of veterans, my grandfather, father, brother, two of my sons, and one daughter-in-law are all veterans. Needless to say, I'm proud to be an American and proud of the service my amazing family has given.

COPYRIGHT

Printed in the United States of America

First published 2018

Fiala, PJ

FINDING HIS FIRE / PJ Fiala

p. cm.

1. Romance—Fiction. 2. Romance—Suspense. 3. Romance - Military

I. Title – FINDING HIS FIRE

ISBN-13: 978-1-942618-48-5